The Dream That Held Us too ... *love that crosses boundaries* ... *about Isa and Ash's love, I fel* ... *making the ordinary, extraordinary. She chooses words* ... *the senses and brings scenes to life with beautiful descriptions that flow like poetry, yet she doesn't shy away from the harsh realities of ageing, loss and fractured relationships. This book carries a universal message about love and finding your way in the world. I adored it.*

Angela Barton - author of *Arlette's Story, Magnolia House* and *You've Got My Number.*

Deeply imbued with a certain wistfulness and haunting sense of loss brought out by the end of a glorious summer, this is an evocative and delicately told story of two young people who meet at Oxford and deeply connect before being abruptly reclaimed by their differ-ent contextual realities and imperatives. Their lives embark on very different courses – though with the passage of time it appears that monotony can be as corrosive for the soul as turmoil. Set in India, Dubai, and England, most notably at Oxford – which has been captured with great feeling and nostalgia – Rhiannon Jenkins Tsang's latest novel is a sensitive and skilful exploration of love, longing, and whether life sometimes relents to give us second chances.

Osama Siddique - author of *Snuffing Out the Moon.*

The Dream that Held Us

First Edition published 2021 by Bunny Publishing.

bunnypublishinguk@gmail.com

Copyright © Rhiannon Jenkins Tsang 2021

The right of Rhiannon Jenkins Tsang to be identified as the author of this work has been asserted by her in accordance with the Copyright, Designs and Patents Act 1988

This is a work of fiction and any resemblance to any person living or dead is purely coincidental. The place names mentioned are real but have no connection with the events in this book

Cover Design by Charlotte Mouncey

Printed in Great Britain by Ingram Sparks

A CIP catalogue record for this book is available from the British Library

ISBN 978-1-8381508-0-8

THE DREAM
THAT HELD US

RHIANNON JENKINS TSANG

BUNNY PUBLISHING

To 'Tea for Five'

Chapter One

Birmingham, September 2010

Isabella had forgotten what he looked like, but never how he made her feel. Dropping the paintbrush, she put her hands over her ears and closed her eyes to block the memory of him. But it came as it always did, a rush of song, colour, smell and sound, the beat of him like tabla drums. No. We can't go back. None of us can. No good ever comes of it. She shook her head in an attempt to dismiss the vision but could not help herself. The memories returned.

They had locked themselves in his cramped college room and were sitting on the bed eating ice cream. He was resting back on the pillow against the wall and she leant against him, cradled between his thighs. He was fresh from the bath, warm and musky, the scent of Old Spice Soap. They held the old half-pint beer glass between them. In it he had made a gargantuan Indian kulfi ice cream. Somehow the tiny galley kitchen at the bottom of their staircase had been bequeathed an old silver spoon. It made the dessert spectacularly indulgent as if they were at The Ritz splashing out money they did not have. He skimmed off the crushed pistachio nuts from the top of the vanilla mound, offering them to her. She supped, but just from the end of the spoon, leaving the rest for him. He licked his lips in anticipation of the cool, wet temptation yet to come.

'Not yet,' he whispered. Slowly, painfully slowly, he mixed the strawberry into the chocolate, at the last moment drawing swirls of smile though the vanilla into the milk.

'Now try!' But then he had become serious, grim almost, feeding her with the spoon as if she were a child. So tender, so kind. God! In that moment, she loved him. But suddenly she was afraid. Something was not right. She felt it. She did not yet know that it was to be their last time together.

The clock in the quad struck five. Together they licked and sipped, the heat of that summer's day dripping off their mouths and the tips of his fingers that trickled like water down her spine. And his voice, thick as late night coffee with cream, soothed and comforted, carrying her to a deep and heavy place.

Picking up her paintbrush, Isabella forced herself back to the present; her little artist's city studio in Birmingham. Half-heartedly, she dabbed spots of yellow over the top of the garden of lavender in her painting. She wanted to make the sunlight run across the tops of the flowers so that the onlooker might imagine them rustling with the summer breeze. But today she could not conjure the wind.

'Damn it!' It had not been going right all day. She wiped her brow with the back of her hand and stood back from the canvas, watching how the light fell. Usually it was the final layer that brought a picture to life, like painting the eyes on a sacred statue. But today she painted like a blind man. The work was meant to be an abstract interpretation of Castle Bolton, a commission for a Singaporean businessman, Mr Lok, who had married a girl from Yorkshire. Unfortunately, the newlyweds had been unable to agree exactly what they wanted so the job had been doomed from the start. Privately, Isabella had given their marriage five years at most. She had suggested painting the castle from the far side of the dale, showing it nestling in the folds of the land, allowing the contours and colours to tell their own story. That was her hallmark style. Mr Lok would have been happy to let her have her way, if it had not been for the young and glamorous Mrs Lok with her half-inch long French-polished nails. Completely missing the point of abstraction, she had insisted that the heads of children in straw hats with blue and pink ribbons must be seen running in the maze garden below the castle. If only that glam-puss knew what motherhood was really like, Isabella now thought, bitter with the day of frustration. At the same time the cautionary words of her agent Alexis, echoed around her head.

'Isabella dear, you must try harder to accommodate your client's wishes. I'm afraid commissions are the price of success. Since that exhibition in New York, they simply can't get enough of you!'

'But not at the price of selling my soul.' She whispered to herself, surveying Castle Bolton with pursed lips.

Yesterday, art students from the local college had come to visit her city garden shed studio. It was an annual event and Isabella had come down early from her main studio in the Yorkshire Dales to host them. With nose rings, tattoos and the lads with pants at half-mast, the aspiring artists were bashful but polite. She told them that her landscape pictures started in her mind as a musical note or pitch, a sound from which colour, form and emotion emerged.

'I'm a failed musician who went to art school after my children were born. I can't compose music so I paint the sounds in my head. I'm at my best when free to paint what a landscape makes me feel.' She had served them tea and pink and yellow Battenberg cake watching which of them kept the marzipan until the end, just as she always did. Asking them about their own work, she was always careful to note the date of their summer exhibition in her diary.

'And don't forget!' she had smiled as she saw them leave down the garden path, 'A good work of art should be a piece of music. It never stands still, never arrives.'

Sighing, Isabella took her rag and began carefully to remove the efforts of the day's labour, taking her picture down to the layer below. Lifting some of the yellow, she saw where she had altered the line of a field wall in her sketch and shortened the shoulder of the dale above the castle. Mary Queen of Scots had been imprisoned there. She imagined the ill-fated Queen in a tatty purple velvet gown, riding out with her guards. A painting is far too much like a life, she thought; layer upon secret layer built up with trial, error and time and best not examined too closely.

Turning away from her canvas, she crashed into her paint table, sending easel, jars and brushes skidding over the wooden floorboards.

'Damn!'

She made no attempt to clear up the mess but went instead to put on the kettle that sat by the old sink in the back corner of the studio. It was a gesture of surrender in the face of a wasted day. Only now as she waited for the water to boil, did she admit the problem to herself. Damn that bloody invitation! Innocuous enough, you might think, in its plush white envelope. It had come from an Oxford University friend Joanna Althrope and her husband Gus. But why now? Why did Joanna's birthday have to fall on that exact weekend? Fate plays a strange hand! Pouring the water, Isabella dunked two tea bags in one large mug, stirred them vigorously with a spoon, then covered the cup with a saucer to let the brew stew. Taking an old rag she got down on her hands and knees to wipe up the mess on the floor. The solvent was already seeping between the floorboards, dragging rivulets of red and black paint from the easel like great tears.

But even the comforting tea-making ritual failed to alter her train of thought that day. Ash Misra! She groaned, doubled up by a rush of pain, panic or was it joy? Don't be so stupid, she said to herself. It was all so long ago. She took a deep breath trying to banish her thoughts; the sticky summer sweat of him, of herself, of them together. She forced herself to think rationally, calmly. Ash Misra. This time she said his name aloud to steady herself. Where on earth could he be in the world today? Perhaps he was an Indian MP. That night lying out in the quad under the stars, he had talked about running for public office. But then again, maybe he had run away from it all and was living in an ashram high in the Himalayas. There had always been a touch of the mystic about him. But of course, he would be married with a gaggle of children. Of that she had no doubt. It might not actually be the case, but over the years she had convinced herself that it would be so. She felt sick to the pit of her stomach. It was always like this when she thought of him, a maelstrom of contradictory emotions. She did not want to remember. But now she no longer had the luxury of pretending to forget. The invitation to Joanna's party, falling by chance on the very weekend he had appointed for them twenty-five years ago, forced her to make a choice. Should she go? If she did, might he be there? And what if he were?

Getting up, she shook her head to clear the fog of memories and restless emotions. One thing is sure, wherever he is, he won't be thinking about me, she thought. His note, little letter, it had been written in haste, in anger. He was bound to have forgotten and most likely she wasn't even remembering it all correctly. And yet, was it not Ash who used to say that they were born under the same star?

Isabella went back to the sink where she had left not just the tea but her Blackberry. Business had taken off to such an extent recently that Alexis had insisted she must have such a device. A cursed thing! She left it switched off most of the time. Removing the saucer from the top of the teacup, she fished out the bags and added two heaped teaspoons of sugar and a large slurp of milk. She liked her tea strong and sweet, Hong Kong milk tea style. It was a habit she had acquired as a teenager in Hong Kong during her father's five year posting there. After her mother died she had taken to bunking off from school to a noodle bar in Causeway Bay. There she would while away the hours drinking cups of the sickly nectar. Picking up the mug of tea and the phone without looking at it, she crossed the studio to stand by the door. She squinted in the sunlight across the lawn towards the house. The leggy summer geraniums still fired red in their pots, but despite the late burst of summer heat, the tips of the leaves on the silver birches were already beginning to turn to copper and gold. Soon she would need to clean the barbeque and harvest her sons' badminton net which sagged limply across the middle of lawn. Shading her eyes, looking north west over the chimney pots, she judged it to be around two thirty; still two hours before she needed to pick up the boys from the station. It was Friday and they had an exeat weekend from school. She decided to shut up shop early. Putting the mobile phone in the back pocket of her jeans, she took a large portfolio folder from the bottom of the bookshelf and seated herself at the little wrought iron table on the veranda of her little studio.

The warm, sweet tea soothed as it trickled slowly down her throat. After a while, she carefully untied the faded blue ribbons of the portfolio, letting the drawings spill out at random onto the table; men and women, naked, of all ages, sitting, crouching, bending, lying, spinning, reaching, dancing. Although Isabella had made a name for herself as an abstract landscape artist in recent years, she had kept her life drawings from art school. She recalled the sittings; the lean, shy ex-coal miner in his mid-eighties who kept his face turned away from the artists. She had just drawn the veins in his hands that were thick blue with dust like swollen rivers. Here was the voluptuous girl with an old penny on a green ribbon round her neck who had lain on the chaise longue dangling her pearl pink slipper on her toes. The table on the veranda wobbled. What if Ash kept his promise? Would the magic still be there? Might a meeting bring closure or something else? The teacup shook in Isabella's hand. Carefully she put it down on the table and bent down to adjust the piece of cardboard under one of the legs.

Righting herself and frowning, she thumbed through her more recent sketches; drawings of a man and a woman sitting on the floor in an embrace. Over and over again she had drawn the man's thigh where it was placed over the woman's, working and reworking the contours of the muscles and the light in the way of hills in her landscape pictures. It was a secret project that she had kept from her inquisitive agent. She wanted to have some pieces of art for herself, away from commercial pressure. The canvases were hidden in her studio in Yorkshire because these experimental endeavours had become her real purpose, an obsession perhaps, and if there is such a thing as peace in this life, she was closest to it in the old farmhouse in Drayburn. Working on these private pieces she was enthralled but strangely free. She had been toiling on the man-woman canvas for years, and she had reached an impasse with the work. But unlike the commissions and commercial pieces, there was no deadline, no pressure to bully something out of herself. She persisted, doggedly determined, driven, quietly picking up her paintbrush whenever she was truly alone, searching the hills with her eyes, revelling in the light, waiting, keeping faith. One day it will come right, she would whisper to herself. I will find what I am looking for, people as mountains of fire and light. I already paint the mountains as if they were alive. One day the two will be one, mountains as people, people as mountains. She knew it for she could hear the idea in her head, far away like a distant drone.

But now the day had come to stillness, the shadows fixed and the drawings lying undisturbed on the table. Leaning back in the chair, Isabella closed her eyes and was afraid. One day, when this painting was finally done, it would be over. She would paint no more.

Chapter Two

Remembering in forgetting, or forgetting in remembering, with Ash Misra she was never sure. As the years passed, things became mixed up in her mind, a crazy patchwork of memories, dim, submerged most of the time. Was it the summer that brought the memory of Ash Misra or the memory that brought the summer she wondered? But one thing was certain, every year for the past twenty-five years on the first day of summer when the bird song swelled to the sky and the pale people raised their surprised heads to welcome the warmth, she remembered him. And always it was that the first day of summer in College that came alive in her mind.

He pounded on the wood of her inner door, barely waiting for her answer and plunged into the heart of her room. She had not been expecting him until the evening. He loomed towards her in his cricket whites, all boy, bat and bag, his head almost touching the ceiling. Was he really that tall, or was it that the room was so small? No matter, for it was the vigour of his youth, their precious youth, that she remembered.

'What a day!' He was panting and dancing from front to back foot as if constantly expecting the next delivery of a ball. Normally she heard him running up the wooden stairs. Taking them in twos and threes, he had a distinctive rhythm, sometimes stopping at her door, other times carrying on up a flight to his own room. This was above Joanna's on the other side of their staircase-G6 Brandon Quad, Woodstock College. Joanna had the room opposite her, and Ash and Li Bin from China had the sets at the top. Ash was four years older than her.

He threw down his kit bag and laid his bat carefully next to her violin which was open in its case on the coffee table.

'Ahh! If England were like this all the time it would be paradise!'

She got up from the desk to greet him, but he reached her first, putting his hands on her shoulders to restrain her, so that she had to stretch up and crane her neck back to take his kiss. He tasted of salt and sunshine, smelt of sweat, linseed oil and freshly mown grass.

'And there are naked women lying about all over the place!' He pulled away, brown eyes wide, waggling his head with laughter.

'Look!' He released her so she could turn back to the desk and look out into the quad. The grubby lead-paned window was ajar, the greater part presenting a crazy vision as if looking at a medieval stained glass. Each of the nine panes housed a slightly different scene, dusty green and blue with jewel-like specks of colour shifting in the golden sun. In the bottom pane Alex Baines and his mates from the boat club had set up the croquet hoops. Engineers and mathematicians by trade, the layout had to be exact, precise, no margin for error. Further along, another group, shirtless, played with a frisbee, spines and shoulder blades sticking out like fish bones from their white flesh. They were still more boys than men. Not far from them, Li Bin strolled down the tired flower trimmed path at the side of the quad. Tall and thin as a beanpole, in need of a haircut, his blue Mao suit trousers were belted high on his waist. As always, it seemed his mind was elsewhere. Through his black rimmed spectacles he seemed neither to look nor see. In the middle panels lay the 'naked women;' girls with their books, the pages flapping in the breeze. Their sun tops, shorts, dresses and skirts were hitched, rolled or pinned above the knees, exposing every possible bit of white flesh to the sunshine. There was only one young man among them, eccentric in a white boater. Felix Thomas. People said he was a talented poet.

'Ash Misra, you are a funny boy! They're only half-naked!' Like Ash, Isabella also saw England through foreign eyes. Born in Karachi, the eldest daughter of a red-headed Scottish civil engineer and Spanish mother, she had grown up abroad; Karachi, Tokyo, Madrid and Hong Kong, always in international schools, always moving on. She belonged everywhere and nowhere. She tweaked Ash's chin and he rested his head on her shoulder to better enjoy the view. His cheek, sticky from an afternoon in the sun, burnt against hers. Her eyes wandered to the top of the window panes. Joanna was sitting in the shade of the sycamore tree surrounded by purple flowers. Her blond head, which bobbed about as she talked, was a good six inches higher than the ginger haired young man already sporting a beer belly, who sat at her side. Will Gregory was his name and apparently he would be Prime Minister one day.

Isabella wondered if he and Joanna were speaking to each other in Greek- as they often did, and felt mildly cross at the thought of it, although she was not exactly sure why. After Freshers' drinks, on the second occasion she had met Ash, smart and formal in his black Nehru jacket, he had politely asked her what language they were speaking, as if he were missing something of great cultural significance. Bizarrely, Isabella had thought of Melissa and Ginnie at the boarding school her father had dispatched her to after her mother had died. The girls would hang out of the window smoking, whispering about the Henley Regatta, Benetton and tickets for Live Aid, but she had not been able to explain what had so irked her about it all.

'Greek as spoken in the English Home Counties!' she had shrugged.

'Not a bad idea. Maybe if we all spoke Sanskrit back home India would be a better place!' He spoke out the corner of his mouth, clipped and short, slightly bitter, and for an instant she thought she saw something else in him; a much older man with a dark shadow under his eyes.

That summer afternoon she felt his breath on the nape of her neck. It smelled sweet and slightly stale. A curl of breeze got round the open window, ruffling the black hairs on Ash's arm. Hidden from the sun, the skin was immodestly white underneath. Gently, as if drawing a veil over something precious, Isabella smoothed the hairs down with the flat of her index finger.

Inhaling the scent of her, he stood up.

'I have a present for you! Close your eyes!'

He went to rummage in his kit bag.

'Don't peep!'

'I'm not!'

'Yes, you are. I can see you!' Coming back, he kissed her on the forehead as if she were a little sister then placed something metallic and cold gently on her neck.

She gasped and pushed him away. Teasing, he tried to drop

it down her front.

'OK! Open now!'

'Coca cola?' she laughed.

'Yes and it's ice cold. I bought a couple of cans from the newsagent on Woodstock Road. Damn Sindhi shopkeeper! 'Yah kya hai? I'm waving the cans under his nose. What kind of bloody rip off price is this brother?' 'It's for my girl. How about special rate for Indians?'

He spoke quickly, Hindi coming out as English, his voice squeaking upwards at the end of the sentence. Laughing at himself, he held a can out in front of him, pulling the ring. It fizzed open and he mopped the excess with back of his hand, licking it off. The second can, he opened more gently, giving it to her.

'Drink!' He tipped his head back. 'Ah! That's good!'

He sat down on the edge of the bed, his knees almost up to his ears.

'Coca Cola is banned in India. It's an import, self-reliance rubbish and all that. Indian Campa Cola is too sweet and, anyway, we are so restrained we always drink it with a straw! But it needs to be drunk like this, rebelliously, indulgently, decadently!' He took a big gulp from the can with his mouth to demonstrate. 'After weddings and parties in India the floor is always littered with straws. If my mother could see me now sitting on a woman's bed drinking from a can!'

'She would say, don't drink so fast, it will give you a pain in your tummy.'

He drained the can in fierce defiance, not of his mother but of something else. She was not exactly sure what but laughed as he licked and smacked his lips in an exaggerated manner.

And then he was looking straight at her, watching her sipping the Coke, wary of the bubbles, curling her tongue round the cold. She had never liked fizzy drinks much but this somehow tasted different with him. He noticed that his box has fallen out of his kit bag and lay next to his helmet on the floor. Suddenly bashful he hurried to zip it back into the bag.

'Can you believe it? In India, when we were young, we didn't even have our own cricket kit. We used to share. Imagine it, with the heat and sweat!' He was making a joke out of embarrassment and she was not sure if he was blushing or if he had caught the sun.

He took his empty Coke can to wash it out in the sink at the far side of the room. Later he would put it on the windowsill in his own room, next to his bottle of Johnnie Walker Red label and a packet of Marlborough cigarettes. Later it would become one of the two things left by him in his abandoned room, a souvenir of that year in the England. She had found them on the day she plucked up courage to say goodbye, only to find that he had already left. The other thing had been a letter, left on his desk, addressed to Isabella. She had read it then torn it up, the tiny pieces falling like snow into his wastepaper basket.

But for the moment he shook the water out of the can and turned it upside down to drain, leaving it next to her toothbrush. Isabella noticed that a stain from where he had polished the cricket ball had bled red into an arc of grass and dirt down the back of his trousers.

'Mucky pup!'

'What?'

'Your trousers.'

He shrugged. 'Nets and fielding drills. I might have taken

a catch or two!' He half-dived and rolled, coming up at her feet, grinning like a two year old who knew he was showing off.

Later still, he twitched quietly, yet violently in his sleep, waking her. At some point he must have pulled the rough blue college blanket over them both. Outside the window a blackbird sang above the crack of a croquet mallet on ball and the gruff shouts of the men in the quad. Raising herself on her elbow she looked at him. His eyelashes were long, almost like those of a girl, a strange contrast to his face which was craggy and thickset with a hooked nose and wide mouth. He slept like a child, every now and then, almost imperceptibly, comfort sucking with his lips. More shouts, laughter and voices. She calculated that it must be late afternoon or early evening with the students already piling out of the library.

He yawned and began to stir, smiling, his eyes still closed.

'We must have dozed off. What time is it?'

She took her watch from under the pillow. 'Five to five.' That left another hour to supper, which was early on a Saturday.

He opened his eyes, stretching the right shoulder where she had laid her head and sat up a little on the pillows.

'Come here!' She put her head down onto his chest, listening to the beat of his heart.

'Play me something!' He looked at her violin at the foot of the bed. 'I've never heard you play.'

'I'm not very good.'

'Just like I'm not very good at cricket!'

'But you are!'

'Good, but not good enough to make a career out of it. Once perhaps, when I was young, but my heart is not really in it in the same way as some of the others in India. They are different to me. I enjoy it, but I want to do other things.' He sighed, and tickled her under the arms, pushing her out of bed, so that she fell, but gently, so he could catch her with his outstretched arm.

'Now play for me!'

She stood with her violin by the music stand, still dressed, for they had never undressed. Yet she felt naked. She reached to close the window so that none of the precious notes would escape into the quad. She was playing Bach's Double Violin Concerto with another student in a teatime concert next week, but now she was shy.

'Don't close the window. Let them hear! I want everyone to hear.' He sat up straight.

'No.' She closed the window shutting out the bird song.

She did not know where to look. At him, at the music? Except that she knew her part by heart. Even so, she adjusted the music on the stand and began to tune up, holding the violin under her chin, arching her arm back to adjust the tuning pegs. It did not need much adjustment for she had practised that morning. She drew the bow, testing A, E, D and G together and back again to the A. All the while she watched him down the length of the strings and over the carved scroll at the top of the neck. He was making himself comfortable, cross legged in the middle of the bed, serious, attentive. She turned slightly to the left to catch his eye. It felt safer that way.

'It's a duet with another violin. You will have to imagine the other part, weaving around like a conversation between two friends. I will play the second movement; the largo.' He nodded, folding his palms in his lap. She hesitated and looked away but he followed her with his eyes, drawing her back.

Tilting her chin, she cradled the violin in its playing position and lifted the bow. Again he nodded, almost imperceptibly this time, as if giving her the cue; a tiny breath, and then he released her.

She pulled out the first phrase with her eyes closed; rich and gentle with just a little vibrato to deepen the tone. Already she had forgotten herself. At the point where the second violin comes in she looked for him. He watched with hooded eyes, his head swaying gently, his face full and calm, and he was a stranger to her, a man from a faraway place. He followed her with soft, circling movements of his body, and followed again, up and over, smiling as the melody died and rose again. Suddenly she stopped. Drained, she could play no more. And yet he was there, holding the tonic note, very quietly with a humming vibration deep in his throat. He sang, without words, in a way she did not know, slowly marking out something around the melody but at the same time stretching it, testing it, easing long slow taut transitions from note to note. It was as if he had picked up her tune, inverted it and somehow collapsed it in on itself. She shivered in wonder. There was a new world that she had never seen, but perhaps had always sensed was there. Tentatively she joined in, slowing her pace, weaving about his line, but it was not a line. He ceded her a few bars but now she felt her music crude and lumpen by contrast. He was travelling again, discovering nooks and crannies. She felt it in the muscles of her neck and shoulders, her chest; opening, swelling and returning, inviting her to catch him where he fell. Her melody was rising, a little louder, her fingers moving up the board, and then it was over. Savouring, she picked out a heavy triplet here and there, and he was sounding a base line, mapping the space beneath, unfolding and refolding pleats of sound like a Jacob's ladder; three dimensions where before Isabella had only imagined one.

From nowhere, the crushing sweet taste of fresh mango oozed in her mouth, the scent of sandalwood wafting on a cotton scarf. In her mind a young woman was making bird mudras with her thumbs hooked together, flying them in the sunshine around her head in a garden. The tops of the woman's hands were hazel brown and her palms white like the camouflage of an owl against a winter sky.

'Bulbul ka bacha, yam yam,' she sang. Gentle wings descended to land on Isabella's little girl cheeks. They were rough and smelt of cooking oil and onions. There was a balcony with stone lattice work like pear drops and a sandstone turret, blood red in the setting sun, and the chant of the muezzin on a jasmine breeze calling to prayer.

Picking up where she had left off, Ash carved a phrase out of nothing, wringing every last possibility from the emptiness. He was in no hurry to get from A to B, and yet the arrival, when it came, was swallowed in an echo deep in his throat. He jutted his chin and smiled, offering it to her with eyes of burnt sugar. Her fear was gone. She tried to follow him, but her notes were too well learned, her fingers clumsy and the gaps on the fingerboard too small. He laughed, and she shrugged, deflecting the challenge by launching full pelt into the final movement of the Concerto. Fast and furious, catch me if you can! He started to clap or was it drum? He marked the rhythms gently at first, the heel of his right hand on the palm of his left and then on his thigh.

'Nah pi, nah pi, tah vi ding! Pink on white, his teeth and

tongue clicked a strange drum language. 'Nah nah ping.'
She realised that while she was playing a tune he was thinking rhythmic cycles, together and apart, together and apart.
Instinctively, she knew where to find him and with a nod and
a grin, always, he was there. Surer now in each other, they
mimicked and teased, louder and faster they played and sang,
until together they stopped somewhere that might have been
the end.

Chapter Three

Oxford, March 1986

'I'm afraid I was a bit of a disappointment to my family. My father and grandfather were both lawyers, although they were musicians by passion.'

Ash's arm was heavy around her shoulders, his waist wide and warm under her arm. She had her thumb crooked into his belt. They had missed supper in College and were walking up to a burger bar in north Oxford to pick up some supper.

'In the end my Dad became such a successful musician that he was able to give up the law and turn professional. It was a terrible scandal at first. It's fine to be an amateur musician in India but professionals are considered low. Then the money started to roll in and my Dad's former colleagues soon changed their tune! He wanted me to follow in his footsteps.'

'What kind of musician is he?'

'He's an Indian classical singer trained in both the Hindustani and Carnatic traditions. He's not famous, but quite well known. He teaches, gives concerts and sometimes works in the movies in Bombay, except that his health is not so good anymore.' Ash was suddenly distracted, preoccupied, his jaw tight, his gaze fixed on the distant bend in the road as if anticipating something, calculating what to do.

'And your Mum?' Isabella tugged gently at his arm. He sighed.

'She's a sitar player, a damn good one. Actually she's better than Ravi Shankar but the men didn't like it so she retired into teaching. It was better that way and she had me and my sister to look after. So you see, music is in my blood, or at least it was supposed to be. When I went to boarding school the music master was so excited.

'Young Misra! You must be in the choir!' But I deliberately did my worst. I just wanted to be outside throwing a cricket ball around. I pretended to sing so out of tune that they soon put me in the back row. In the end they threw me out of the choir!'

The low heels of Isabella's court shoes tapped on the pavement and she realised they were walking in step. They began to make a game out of avoiding the cracks in the pavement, stepping together into the centre of the next stone. Except that his stride was wider than hers so he could cross two stones with ease.

'Music is my escape,' Isabella said as she hopped to keep up. 'My family was never very stable. My father was an adventurer and workaholic. My Mum, well, she was unpredictable and there were always rows. Sometimes we were barely a year in one place. In the end it was easier not to bother to make friends, just play the violin, draw and paint or go to Mass. The church was always quiet with ritual, routine and certainty. Wherever I was in the world, whatever was going on at home it was the same. I liked that.' She squinted up at Ash and noted that he was listening. He didn't always. Sometimes his attention would wander just as it had done a minute previously. It was as if he were suddenly distracted by a matter of great concern. His brow would furrow and the sparkle go out of his eyes. Isabella now judged it her turn to confess.

'My Mum might have been a good artist if she had not married my Dad and slowly pickled herself yellow with drink in expat clubs. She was considered a great beauty when she was young, a muse to some, or so they said. But I used to squirm with embarrassment at her old stories. She would waft her cigarette and tell anyone who would listen about, 'when I was living in Paris' and 'my dear friend, Pablo Picasso.' She died in Hong Kong when I was fifteen. Dad bundled me off to boarding school in the UK after that. I don't blame him. I wasn't the easiest teenager in town, too independent, not keen on rules. I was a born loner; the only child of two self-centred only children. I've always had to fight to forge my own way. If my mother had had what she wanted I would have ended up in finishing school in Switzerland, not here at Oxford. She had quaint nineteenth century ideas about my upbringing; riding lessons, ballet lessons, music and art, but a lady should not be too clever, and certainly never outshine her man!' Isabella stopped. She did not want to tell Ash that by the end her mother's face was chafed red and distended like an old soak twice her age, but still she had insisted on having her eyebrows plucked and her hair back-combed in a ridiculous 1960s style. She remembered her lying in her hospital bed with her swollen feet propped up on a pillow like glove puppets. And always her nicotine stained fingers reaching for a cigarette and lipstick, followed in due course by the clicking of her rosary beads.

'I don't want a life like my mother's.' Isabella said quietly. Ash nodded, leaving the rhythm of their marching feet as response.

'Ki ta, ki ta ki tata,' he sang their footstep beats.

They had left behind most of the central Oxford colleges. The streets were narrower now, poorer, deserted, except for a robin which hopped along in front of them. They could see into the front rooms of some of the tiny terraced houses, dormant fireplaces, white painted bookshelves in alcoves filled with books, and old lady knitting.

Ash picked up the conversation.

'My Dad and I never got on. It's been worse over the last few years. Poor health makes him bad tempered and me guilty. Funny thing though. In the end the music helped with the cricket and the cricket got me the India Scholarship to Oxford. Then, oh my God, Dad was proud! He jiggled his head and waved his hands in an imitation of a celebratory dance. 'My parent's families came as refugees from Lahore in 1947. They had to start over with nothing. My Dad made a good fist of things financially, but without the scholarship, we couldn't have afforded it.' He looked at her to see if she had understood. She had but not fully. All the same, he smiled at her and that made her heart leap.

'Batting and bowling, you see. Even the rhythm of the day when you are standing out there on the field, it's all in the raag, the tala and the bol- the melodies, rhythmic cycles and language of the tabla. My Uncle is a tabla player, the Indian drums. Night and day there were always musicians in our house, Hindus, Muslims, some Sikhs too. My Dad used to joke that this was the way India was meant to be! They were always making music. I suppose some of it must have rubbed off on me. For me each bowler has his own run up patterns. It's a bit like tabla players who play with different fingers and styles. It's hardly orthodox cricket and I would never admit it to my old man. But when I bat I don't just watch the bowler. I actually hear the run ups like tintal, or beat patterns with different bol or word beats in their feet. Each bowler has his own individual rhythm, like a signature tune.' He let her go and began to run slowly across the street, curling his bowling arm with an imaginary ball

'Dha, dhin, dhin dha, dah tin tin ta!' His arm reached as if releasing the ball straight at the evening sun. 'The crucial thing is the timing from the moment of release, the cycle, that way I can anticipate the speed and direction of the ball.'

'Ki ta ta, ki ta, ki ta, kit ta ta, ki ta, ki ta' His tongue clicked words and beats at speed and she ran to keep up. Out of breath and laughing they arrived at the burger bar. Putting his arm around her, he took her inside.

The clocks had gone forward to summer time bribing the sun to hang on into the evening. When they got back into central Oxford the streets were still warm. The light illuminated the tops of the buildings in desert red and gold, casting shadows of pyramids and triangles on the walls and across the streets. They hurried so that the burgers did not get cold.

'Look!' Isabella pointed to the round open-sided Indian style turret with its little cap top on the corner of Hertford College. 'I have never noticed it before.'

'Perhaps you Imperialist Brits pilfered it from the Red Fort at Agra. It might even have canon ball holes in it! Not to worry. It is only a small turret. No one will miss it!' He pulled her close to him and waved to Taff, the porter, in their college Lodge.

They turned left down in the dark passage that stored bikes and ran from the front to the back quad. It was too narrow for them to walk abreast because of the bikes against the wall; decades, a century even, of abandoned metal skeletons. He put his hand on her shoulders to steady her as she walked in front. Suddenly, for the first time in her life she felt at home somewhere, here in a college passage, with him.

He had both their burgers stuffed up the front of his cricket jumper to keep them warm. At the door to his room he rested his hand on his belly like a pregnant woman, fiddling the key into the lock.

Once in the room he threw open the window and they sat cross legged on the floor opposite each other and ate. The burgers were sweet and fatty. Ketchup, tomatoes, onions and gherkins alternately and together attempted to escape from the sides of the buns as they bit down. He joked about his mother and the fact that he was eating beef.

After a while she said, 'When I was playing my violin this afternoon I remembered something from my childhood. Did I tell you that I was actually born in Karachi when my Dad had a work project there? I had a nanny called Meena and there was a garden with a mosque nearby. She used to sing me a song about a bird called *Bulbul Ka Bacha*. It's strange, I remember the words but not the meaning.

'It's Urdu not Hindi but I understand.'

'Bulbul ka bacha, Khata tha khichri,' Isabella sang quietly.

'The Nightingale's baby, would eat cereal.' He scooped a falling onion ring from her bun with his little finger and offered it back to her.

'Gata tha ganay, Meray sirhanay.' Her words were muffled, mumbled.

'Would sing songs, sitting by my head.'

She wiped a drop of ketchup from his chin and licked her finger.

'Main ne uraya, Wapas na aaya.'

I made him fly away. He didn't come back.'
'Bulbul ka bacha.'
'The Nightingale's baby.'

CHAPTER FOUR

Birmingham, September 2010

The lunch invitation, printed on expensive white card with nuptial blue writing, lay exactly where Isabella had left it earlier that morning; in the middle of the kitchen island worktop. The purple skin from the onions she was preparing to go with the sausages for supper, fluttered down around it, settling like petals. Damn it! Joanna's birthday! Of all the weekends!

Joanna and Gus Althrope request the pleasure of Mr and Mrs Anthony Harrington and family for lunch to celebrate Joanna's birthday.
Strictly no presents.

Isabella's onion-teared eye wandered to the bottom of the invitation.

RSVP The Right Hon Joanna Althrope MP
House of Commons, Westminster.

Beneath it Joanna had scribbled in rounded schoolgirl hand writing that had tended to go more and more downhill over the years.

Bring boys and wellies. Stay over? Let me know. Bit of a full house. XX Jo.

PS Can you believe it? 25 years since we first went up to Oxford this autumn. Lots of the old crowd. You absolutely MUST come!

Reaching for the chopping board Isabella looked at the clock then out of the window down the lane. She couldn't help herself. Her twins, Ferdie and Jamie, had been away at boarding school for several years now, but every day at that time her heart twisted into a knot. She still watched out for them, coming home from the local school as they used to do. There would have been one of two scenarios. Either the boys would have been walking together the best of friends or Ferdie would have been trailing behind, his face as black as thunder, shoulders hunched, dragging his feet, eyes on the ground. Poor Ferdie, he was the elder twin by two minutes, but it was always Jamie that apparently effortlessly excelled at everything at school, rugby, cricket, cross country, music, form prizes, while Ferdie, try as he might, lagged behind. She had not wanted them to go to a boarding school at all and had fought tooth and nail to prevent it. But her husband, Tony, and his family had insisted. Generations of Harrington boys had gone to the school and the twins should follow in their father's, grandfather's and great grandfather's footsteps. When they first went away, Isabella had cried herself to sleep at night and worried herself ragged, especially about Ferdie. Unlike other women whose boys went off to prestigious public schools, she was not even able to take solace in a vicarious pride that her children had made it through the entrance examinations with all the implied promise of long term glory and success that attendance at such hallowed institutions implied. For her the whole thing was a great pretence. The twins would have done just as well at the local school.

But she had lost the war with Tony and their relationship had not been the same after the boys left. They had both retreated into their own lives, passing like ships in the night. Work had always been Tony's priority, just has it had for her father, and her husband had never really had time for Isabella. Painting filled the gap in her life. Out of her loneliness and depression had come her best pieces, paradoxically saving her, she admitted to herself, from her mother's fate.

Chop, chop, chop. Isabella's eyes streamed. Perhaps all marriages are a disappointment, she thought. We expect too much of them, of each other. Maybe it is the way of things? Chop, chop, chop. She was quick with the knife and soon the onions were done. The Skype on the computer in the hall called. Sniffing and wiping her hands on her apron, Isabella went over and clicked the mouse.

Tony was in Beijing on business, again. He sat formally in front of his computer like a child having a passport photo taken. Except he was too tall and the top of his head appeared to have outgrown the screen.

'Hello!' he said sheepishly and waited for her to take the initiative with the conversation. Except that she wasn't in the mood to play along.

'Hiya!'

'Boys back yet?'

'Nope. I'm fetching them from the station at four.' Isabella felt herself raging quietly deep inside. Tony wouldn't be home for the weekend. His absence did not matter to her. She was way past that but she did care for the boys' sake. And then there was the suspicion that he had chosen to stay away that nagged and gnawed.

'How are they?'

If you were home you could ask them yourself. It was on the tip of her tongue to let rip, but right then she hadn't got the energy to pick a fight.

'Fine. Ferdie got selected for the rugby A team, at last! It provoked the usual one-upmanship.'

Tony shrugged.

'That's great. I'm really pleased. Boys, you know Bella! They're bound to compete.' Another supressed niggle inside. She had never liked him calling her Bella. Her preferred diminutive, if there had to be one, was Isa.

'As long as the two of them don't murder each other now they're in the same team!' She attempted a joke. But already the conversation was petering out. It was late in China, and Tony wore the blue and white cotton pyjamas she had bought him last Christmas from his favourite London tailor. He was abroad more and more these days. His clients had factories all over the world, and when he came home he was jet lagged and sat in front of the television watching sport. She stared at the skinny bald business executive with rimless spectacles on the screen. He looked like a middle-aged Milky Bar Kid. How could it be that you spend twenty years with someone and one day he turns into a total stranger? When did it happen? When is it that we become middle aged? Unlike his contemporaries who had got fat with business travel and corporate meals, Tony remained lean except that all the colour seemed to have bleached out of him. He sat in front of a mist of hotel net curtains. His once blond hair had diminished to a few strands of grey that he brushed over his bald patch in the same direction as his father used to do; old, tired, eaten up. She wondered how he saw her, his Trouble and Strife. A middle aged house wife, red eyed from the onions, with a sagging chin? She was the one who badgered him to put the dates of the boys' school events in his diary, to take holidays and not to work so hard.

'Why do you have to work so much? It's not as if we need the money anymore. There's enough in the trust to see the boys through and my paintings are selling really well, especially since the Americans started buying. Why don't you let a colleague do some of the long haul business trips and spend more time with the boys?' But he would never listen.

'How was your day?' Tony asked.

'Fine.' She had long since stopped talking to him about her 'doodles' as he called them. Suddenly her head spun, the screen scattering into a hail of tiny diamonds. Taking a deep breath, she broached the subject.

'Joanna and Gus have invited us all to party at Farndon; the first Saturday in October.'

'That's a bit last minute, isn't it?'

'It's her birthday.' Isabella said nothing about the coincidence of the birthday and 25 years since matriculation at Oxford. She shuddered and there was a lump in her throat. 'Actually, I think Gus is looking for an excuse to distract Jo from the expenses scandal. I don't have to go.'

'Huh!'

Tony paused to scratch his nose and picked at his left nostril as was his habit.

'Bit off if you don't go, though, given the situation. Bloody MPs! Line the lot of them up against a wall and shoot them. You go if you want to. I don't want to come.'

'But we could go together, have a romantic weekend.' Isabella said brightly. 'Joanna and Gus were very kind to us when the twins were small. Perhaps they need a little back from us right now?'

'Tosh, Bella. Those sorts of people are only interested in themselves and I really don't want to go. I am in London all week that week; wall to wall meetings and...'His voice was rising and Isabella pre-empted the rest of the conversation. She knew how it would go.

'Ok. It doesn't matter. I'll say no.'

He sighed with fatigue.

'I think you should go, after all they're your friends, not mine. Why don't you use some of my air mile credit and book yourself into the Rexeter in Oxford? Then you don't have to stay in that draughty old country house. Bloody Gus is so tight he won't double glaze the place and it's always freezing, even in the summer. Make a weekend of it, why don't you, dear?

The dear was a too obvious add-on. For a few seconds it hung in cyber space, a thread of something that once had been between them. Then Tony smiled and his voice softened.

'It would do you good to get out of that damn studio. You're alone in Droverdale far too much. I might even drive over to school to watch the boys play rugby while you're away. It will do me good to puff up and down the touch line after them, and you're always telling me I need to spend more time with them.'

The Skype beeped and the line dropped. She thought she heard him say, 'I love you,' and messaged back.

'Take care.'

So it was decided, at least in part, and Tony was right about one thing. She had two exhibitions coming up, a preview in

Drayburn in Yorkshire in October, and then a big one in New York in the New Year. A break would do her good.

CHAPTER FIVE

Isabella hurried off to the station to fetch the twins. They were soon home. The back door slammed and they loped into the kitchen like hungry hounds. Throwing their black rucksacks onto the floor, they kicked off their shoes, stripped off their jackets and headed straight for the toaster where Isabella ambushed them for kisses. They were tall like their father but had a few of her own father's Scottish genes making them broader across the shoulders and gloriously red-headed like her. They bent down to kiss her on the cheek, dutifully, for she needed it more than they did.

'What's for supper Mum?'

'Hotpot with crispy potatoes.'

'Yum.'

'When's Dad going to Skype?' Jamie asked, all bright-eyed.

Isabella took a deep breath. Her heart ached for him.

'He rang an hour or so ago. It's late in Beijing. You'd better hurry if you want to catch him before he goes to sleep.

Jamie disappeared into the living room with his mobile phone leaving Ferdie at the kitchen island spreading marmite and peanut butter on the toast. She could see the anger, hurt and pain on his face.

'Your Dad, loves you, you know.'

He didn't reply.

She had been struggling to keep a line of communication open between Tony and boys for years. But it was a losing battle. They had so little to talk about anymore and when Tony was home he chose to assert himself and throw his weight about which was not a good strategy for the teenage boys.

Isabella changed tack.

'How's school? Any juicy gossip for your old Mum?'

'Yeh. All good.' He would tell her more later, in due course, so Isabella bided her time. Ferdie was the sensitive one and had struggled to adapt to boarding school life. It had broken her heart to see him build walls around his emotions in order to survive.

'I'm going to Godmother Joanna's in Oxford for a lunch party the first Saturday in October. Dad says he might come over to school to watch the rugby.' Isabella said brightly.

'Whatever,' Ferdie paused then changed the subject. 'Jamie should make her some of his rum truffles for you to take to Farndon. Godmother Joanna really likes those. It might cheer her up' He stuck two pieces of toast together and took a big bite. 'You know, with everything on the news and all.'

Isabella smiled. 'Don't worry. Godmother Joanna will be fine.' But she wasn't entirely sure she believed it, for the press had their knives out and Joanna Althrope MP was high on their list.

Ferdie turned to get a plate from the cupboard, put his sandwich on it, then bent and shouldered his rucksack.

'Mum, I've got a load of homework and I want to get it out of the way. Give me a shout when you want me to lay the table.'

After supper Isabella was in the utility room. She heard

the boys clearing the table and stacking the dishwasher in the kitchen. Their voices gruff and grunting, they talked a young man's banter, a language she did not always understand. She hung the last of the laundry on the Sheila Maid drying rack and hauled the rope to pull it up to the ceiling. The weather was hot. The six o'clock news had declared an Indian summer. Her jeans and t-shirts would be dry before morning.

By the time she returned to the kitchen the boys had left. Everything was in its place. She had got them well trained. She stood with her palms flat on the cool marble of the kitchen worktop, steadying herself. Everything might be in order, yet something had changed. She padded over to Tony's wine rack on the far side of the kitchen, her bare feet making no sound. She had made it a rule never to drink alone. Sniffing at the risk, she pulled out a small two-glass bottle of Rioja, turned the screw cap and poured half a glass. The bottle was too small even to offer a proper glug. She sipped, cautiously wetting her lips with oak and tannin, as if she were smoothing on lipstick. Opening the kitchen door she crossed the hall. Jamie lay on the sofa watching *Top Gear*. His left foot crossed over his right, hung off the far end in exactly the same way as did his father's. There was a hole in his sock.

'When was the last time you cut your toe nails Jamie?' Isabella nagged and wished she had not.

He harrumphed and turning his head, spotted he glass of wine.

'You alright Mum?'

'Yes, fine.'

In the dining room next door Ferdie had started trumpet practise. He launched full blast into *Mack the Knife*. He knew it was Isabella's favourite and that made it difficult for her to tell him to tone it down.

'Mum, can't you tell Ferdie to put a sock in it? I swear he plays that bloody tune just to wind me up!'

'Language!'

Another harrumph.

Closing the door to the living room and then the dining room, Isabella climbed the stairs to Tony's study. She closed that door too.

Sitting at her husband's desk, her fingers pitter pattered across the computer keyboard, lightly and easily. She imagined a shower of calming summer rain.

Dear Jo and Gus,

Thank you so much for your invitation to the matriculation lunch. I would love to come. Tony will be just back from Beijing (again, poor thing) so sends his apologies as do the boys. They are in school that weekend and can't escape the rugby tyranny. I won't stay over this time. Do let me know who else is coming!

Much love Isa.

PS Chin up and big hug. It will all blow over soon. I am sure.

She hit send and it was a done deal. She was going to Farndon and that meant she would be near Oxford that weekend, that Sunday.

Leaning back in Tony's big black desk chair, she sipped again on the wine. Through the open window, she watched without seeing; the pigeons chatting on the garden fence, the children jumping on the trampoline in the neighbour's garden and somewhere down at the bottom of the road a dog barked.

Would Ash come to Joanna's lunch? Was it likely? Last she had heard, no one knew what had happened to him or if they did they weren't saying. In all the years she had known Joanna and her gang, no one had ever mentioned Ash Misra. Strange, for the rest of them had all kept more or less in touch, looking over their paranoid, ambitious shoulders, each clocking the progress of the others; houses in Kensington and Chelsea, Windsor, the Dordogne, the Algarve, a brace of children in private school, rungs chalked off on the corporate ladder. After the twins were born when Tony had got a partnership at a Birmingham firm and they had moved out of London, people had whispered.

'I am so sorry. It must be so hard.' Isabella was going north! In their minds this was social suicide. It was only after her agent set up her first exhibition in London that invitations started to arrive once more. By then she couldn't give a damn. She supposed the same applied to Ash Misra. For the others, he was a brief encounter in their narrow Oxford lives. He just wasn't useful to them in their vain London corporate and political worlds. So he was forgotten. It was as if he had never existed and yet in the recesses of Isabella's heart, something lived on. It made her uneasy, put her on edge. In truth, it terrified her. What was it; a thirst, a lust, a need, a sin? She had never understood it and had always mercilessly kicked the tangle of sensations and emotions about that period of her life to the back of her mind. But whatever it was it had already nearly destroyed her and she feared it had the power to tear her life apart once again. And yet, already it, Ash, him, them, the dream that held them, was reeling her in. She was like a fish caught in a net, struggling, gasping for air, resisting with all her might.

The wine glass was empty. She topped it up with the rest from the bottle and crossed the room to open a cupboard. It was full of boxes of photographs, albums and rows of photo CDs. All had been meticulously labelled and filed by Tony over the years. He was obsessively precise in everything he did which caused Isabella to feel messy and disorganised, which was not actually the case. *Normandy Summer 95, Three Peaks 2000, Twins' Christening,* he had printed in neat black capitals on red leather photograph albums. She pulled out *Wedding 1990* and giggled at the ridiculous vision of her veiled self in a puff ball meringue dress in the style of Princess Diana. Her hair was done in a French pleat and she stood on the arm of her father at the door to Winchester Cathedral. Her Dad had nearly not come to the wedding because his second wife, a Hong Kong girl not much older than herself, had been eight and a half months pregnant at the time. Isabella flipped through some of the other pages and boxes; Tony beagling with his mates from Cambridge, and the two of them at Ascot the summer before they had got married. It was clear to her why she had loved him. He was the quintessence of Englishness. He had never doubted his place in the world and until the last ten years or so had never had much need to look beyond the UK for business. He had offered her a certainty and stability that her parents' nomadic life had never done. She had wanted to belong somewhere, to be part of something and he had given her a place in the world to call home. Without him she would not have had the house in Drovedale where she found so much solace and inspiration. Isabella flipped another page of an album. Here she was on her wedding day again standing with Tony and the Cathedral choir dressed in scarlet, the choristers' medals glinting in the summer sun. The bottom shelf was labelled *Misc*. There Tony had put Isabella's family photographs, the ones taken of her early life as a child and before they met. And there it was. Left loose, in the back of a large black album with a gold embossed rose on the front, Isabella found the one picture she had of Ash Misra. It had never been labelled or stuck in.

Outside, the neighbour's dog had fallen silent and the birds had shut up shop. The light faded and all was still. With it came the long lost sense of a vastness inside herself and it was as if she were falling, tumbling, tumbling down. It had been like that when she had first seen Ash twenty-five years ago in the Lodge at College. He had been a young man fresh off the plane from India who had made an ass of himself. But even then, in that instant, she had known he would change her life. She knelt on the floor, covering her eyes to control the collapsing sense of weakness and the rush of colour which was her memory of their last day together.

The red roof tiles on the pavilion were pale with sun, the green of the trees and the cricket pitch was not really green at all but blue. The breeze ruffled the pages of Isabella's neglected book, the yellow topped daisies pranced round the outfield, and the dandelion seeds floated like tiny jellyfish before her eyes. The only colours that were certain were the pink, orange and red spots of the girls' dresses sitting on the pavilion balcony. Drugged by heat and lethargy, Isabella lay on her front under a great yew tree. Its long black shadow played as strands of seaweed on a shore around one of the fielders on the boundary.

She had chosen that spot at lunch in order to do some revision for her examinations and watch the cricket at the same time. A cooing dove marked time with the soft thud of the bowler's feet. The bird seemed to know exactly when each over began and ended. The ball cracked on the bat, flying high into the blinding blue sky.

'Catch!' the fielders called.

Isabella felt too hot to move, and Ash had been out in the middle for hours. He had gone in at number three in the final innings when Oxford University was trailing by one hundred and seven. Patient, unnoticed at first, he took his shots, letting his partners have their head, batsmen thumping glove against glove as the runs came and went. The minutes passed and Ash took over more and more on strike. He was a magician, Isabella thought. How did he do it, conjure time and space out of speed and with it runs? He never hunched over his bat or tensed up, was never in a rush. He moved with complete economy and total control, whatever the bowlers threw at him. It is like when I am with him, she thought. There was an opening up, a creation of the new between them, an ease and simplicity of something that was meant to be. A ripple of distant applause; he drove a four between the covers to the boundary, and hooked the next ball for six over short leg. The sun was high in the sky and there was a heat about him now, a grim determination. Not only was he batting for victory, she thought, but battling that something else that hidden thing that preyed upon him. She had had glimpses of it over the past year when his mood suddenly shifted and he had become distracted, introspective. She had probed, gently, but without success. Only once had she thought he was about to reveal himself, but he had pulled back.

Whatever it was, it remained hidden, obscure, troubled, known only to him. Again the bowler prowled round the wicket, but Ash reeled him in, as if he had the ball on a rubber string. He was the master now, the centre of the universe. The fielders, bowlers, they all revolved around him. He sent another ball down to deep-mid wicket.

'Yes,' he shouted and the batsmen took a quick two.

Isabella knew all the names of the fielding positions, of the batsmen's stances and shots, of the bowlers' delivery techniques; Yorkers, googlies, leg and off breaks, silly mid-off, silly mid-on. One cold dark winter's night to take his mind of things, Ash had drawn her pages of charts; diagrams in red and green for exactly where the bowler might place the ball, pencil stickmen on the front foot and the back foot, hooking, sweeping and driving, field placements drawn and redrawn for left hander and right handers. He talked as a shy poet, out of the corner of his mouth, streams of rich clickety clack words, his 'w's pronounced as soft 'v's, his 'ds' merging with his 't's and when he got excited his voice would rise upwards at the end. His bowling hand too was always warm whilst hers was cold. He curled it round hers and over the faded, loose seamed old cricket ball he had brought with him from India.

'Like this to bowl leg spin. Two fingers down, right to left as if you are opening a door.' The ball thudded against the closed bedroom door. At that time he was still injured and she had fetched the ball. 'And the googly, the wrong'un is like this, out of the back of the hand. You have to watch the bowler's hand or you don't read it right.'

'Cricket, it's like chess. Many different ways to move the pieces.'

He had adjusted his position on the bed, winced with pain and smiled. 'When I'm out on the field I think of nothing but the game. I am free.'

That warm day Ash was ninety one not out at stumps. The Oxford men punched the air and ran in to congratulate their man of the match. Ash had missed his century but they had won. Thinking that he would want to be with the boys for a while, Isabella slowly packed her bag and strolled over to the pavilion. They were all at the bottom of the steps, shaking hands with the opposing team, drinking water and beer, hugging each other and slapping shoulders. Ash turned away from them laughing, bat in hand, cap in the other and she saw that he was looking for her. It was at that moment she had taken the photograph. As the others were leaving to climb the steps to the dressing room, the shutter snapped just as he caught sight of her and before she reached him. A moment of perfection she had thought would last forever.

He reached out and put his arm round her, kissing her on the cheek, and very briefly, proprietarily on the mouth. Then he drew her up the pavilion steps.

'I want to show you off to the boys,' he whispered.

'I'll see you later? Don't you want to go and have a drink and celebrate your win?'

'No,' his response was curt, abrupt, suddenly desperate almost threatening. But then he smiled. 'Isabella, tonight I want to eat ice cream with you.'

In the tiny galley at the bottom of their staircase in College that counted as a kitchen, he was gentle, too gentle, later she knew why. He stood behind her nuzzling her neck.

'Like this!' He put pistachio nuts in a plastic bag and taking the back of a battered old saucepan, smashed and ground them into small pieces.

'Come with me!' He nipped the shoulder of her summer dress with his teeth, unintentionally catching a little skin, dragging her like a puppy to the fridge. Taking out a bottle of rose cordial, he handed it to her and dived into the small partly iced up freezer compartment to grab the two little tubs of ice cream. Not letting go of her, he manoeuvred round, pressing against her to hold the freezing boxes between their chests as he took a pint of milk. It was an eccentric embrace and they laughed.

'First you put in the rose cordial into the bottom of the glass, like so! He poured an inch of the bright pink syrup. 'And then you add the milk and stir. And now the ice cream, chocolate, strawberry and vanilla.' He scooped great round lumps with a dessert spoon, 'One, two, three, are you hungry? His eyes were teasing and wide as if he were talking to a child. 'Now you do the honours and sprinkle the nuts on the top.'

The ice cream was gone. They had scraped the inside of the glass clean with the old silver spoon. It had not been polished for years and was oxidized black. They were resting together on the bed and he leant back to open the small lead-paned window above his head. Coyly at first, the breeze tugged a little at the blue curtains, creeping down at length from the windowsill to caress and entwine their legs and arms. Gently, the curtains opened and closed, scattering random tides of black and white mosaic. His face was half in shadow half in the light. The curtain hooks rattled and the shadow of a bird danced over their bodies

At length Isabella said, 'You were so beautiful today!'

He smiled without opening his eyes, stroking her bare shoulder.

'It is not I who was beautiful but you! I was just lucky. The wicket was a dead one. It favoured me. The bowlers couldn't do that much with it and they lacked a real spinner. Life is all about luck.'

They were silent for a while. In her room below, Joannna was running a political meeting, her deep plummy tones like blotting paper absorbing, the voices of the others. From the set opposite came the sound of Li Bin playing Chinese pop on his tape recorder.

'Li Bin's an odd one.' Isabella said.

'Hmmm! I'm not surprised. He's on a Chinese government scholarship. Not much money. Even less than me, and the bastards are keeping his wife and baby daughter as hostages back in China to ensure he goes home when he graduates.'

'That's terrible.' Isabella said. 'I had no idea.'

But Ash was not really listening. His changed tone, suddenly serious.

'Isabella, I need to talk to you.' She did not see it coming. Their future was already planned out in her mind. They had discussed it. He would finish his Master's at the end of the following year and get a job with a merchant bank in London. They would be together. She had never doubted it. For the first time in her life, with Ash, everything had been right.

'Next year,' he said it quickly. 'It will be different.'

His body stiffened, waiting for her response.

She raised herself on her elbow. He had opened his eyes but was staring at the ceiling.

'My father is ill. He has cancer of the pancreas. He's not long for this world.' He pushed a long strand of hair back behind her ear and smoothed her forehead. 'It's his dying wish.'

'What is?' And then she saw it, as in the moments before a car crash. 'No, no, no,' she screamed inside. 'Don't do this to me!'

He looked away saying it quickly to get it over with.

'Next year I will be in married quarters. I will be bringing my wife.'

The world was falling apart, spinning out of control. She tried to grab it back, but it was too late. Her heart gave one heavy thump then missed a beat.

'You're married?' She heard a voice speak from within herself but it was not her own.

'No. But I will be this summer. My mother has found a girl from a good family for me and I have said yes.'

'What?' Isabella's mouth was open and for a few seconds there was no breath to make more words. 'How long have you known about this?' She croaked. 'So you've been lying to me all this time? '

'No, Isa, it's not like that. You have to believe me. It was only decided recently. I only got the letter last week. I've been trying to find a good time to tell you. ' Getting up and putting on his shirt, he took a blue airmail envelope from his desk drawer, offering it to her. She slapped it out of his hand.

He tried again. 'My mother says it is her greatest duty to find me a good wife.' But it sounded weak and he knew it.

'I don't believe you and I don't want to know.' She was putting her dress on struggling with the zip and he came to help her.

'Please, please, just listen.' He reached to touch her shoulder.

'Isa sit down. You don't understand' She pushed him away.

'I understand very well. You are having an arranged marriage and you have lied to me. Have you met the girl?'

'Not yet. Actually there are two lined up. One is a back-up so to speak. The wedding date is fixed for August. I am sorry.' He sat down heavily on the edge of the bed, his head in his hands.

She stood in the middle of the room, hands on hips.

'Are you seriously telling me you are going to marry a girl you've never met or possibly the back up? Have you gone insane?'

'It's the Indian way. Family first, always family first.' He could not meet her eye.

Desperately, Isabella tried another tack. 'Ash, you don't have to do this. You are your own boss. For heaven's sake, this is the twentieth century. Don't you love me?'

'You know I do.' His voice cracked, the sun went in and the shadow of the bird disappeared from the room.

Tears poured down Isabella's cheeks. Quickly she wiped them away. She was angry and did not want him to see her cry.

'Can't you tell your family that you love me? We could go to America together or I could come back to India with you. If we love each other, that will be more than enough. It's nothing to do with the families.'

'No, it's impossible. ' He shouted and stood up, fists balled, teeth clenched, and she was afraid of his height and strength. He wiped his nose with the back of his hand. 'You're young, Isabella. There are lots of things you don't understand.'

'Don't understand? How dare you? Why don't you try and explain?'

He sighed, infuriated, angry, exhausted.

'I have never told you but my Grandfather was a Member of the Congress Party, an activist before Independence. He was imprisoned three times by the British. It ruined his health. And my Grandmother has never forgiven Mountbatten for what he did to Lahore. The announcement over which side the city would go to came so late. They waited and waited in the hope it would go to India. Her sister was dragged off by a gang of Muslim men and never heard from again. Perhaps the family would have left earlier if they had known.' He dithered from one foot to another but this time looked as if did not know how to play the ball. 'Ever since she arrived in Dehli, every day of her life as long as I can remember, my Grandmother began it with her prayer beads and by cursing Mountbatten, the last Viceroy of India. Do you know, when he was blown up in that boat by the IRA, she did a dance of joy in front of the television; whooping and whirling round the living room like a crazy Bhadrakali, her false teeth in one hand, roti pan in the other.

'You see! You see! All these years I have been praying for revenge. Bad karma. It catches up with you in the end!'

Ash stared at Isabella looking for a reaction but she gave him none. He pressed on, ramming home the point, 'And my mother! She is very devout. Isabella, she wouldn't even eat with you. I wax lyrical about my father and his Muslim musician friends because that is the way he and I want it to be. But if I tell you the truth, my Mum chucks them all out to the bazaar to eat because she still believes that Muslims are unclean. Isabella, you have no idea, and our children, our children would be…'

'What mixed race?' What's the shame in that?'

'Isabella, trust me. I am older and wiser. One day you will

thank me for this.'

'How dare you patronise me like this. It's pathetic.' She spat out the words.

'Pathetic! Don't you dare call my family pathetic,' he shouted.

'I'm not calling your family pathetic. It's you who is pathetic. His was furious now.

'You have no idea what happened to us because, because…'he stuttered with fury. 'Because of the British. My Grandmother walking thousands of miles with two small children in tow. I've never seen our family home in Lahore, imagine that!' His face swelled red with rage and he took a step towards her.

'Don't even think about hitting me!' She raised her right arm to protect her face and he backed away. 'It's a cop out and you know it. Far too easy to blame everything on the British because…because you are a coward.'

Coward! The word echoed around the room and Ash reeled from it as if she had landed him a killer blow. The blood drained from his face but she was glad of it. How she wanted him to hurt him, to make him hurt as much as she was hurting, not just to twist the knife but to hack again and again deep into the marrow of his soul. She picked up her bag and turned to leave the room.

'I never want to see you again.'

'Isabella, wait!'

But she had not looked back.

Twenty-five years later, sitting on the floor in Tony's precision tidy study, Isabella's tears flowed again. Now she made no attempt to wipe them away. At the time she had thought Ash was angry, but now as an older woman she read his reactions as born of fear and confusion and something else, that she still even after all these years she did not fully understand.

They had parted like that and she had never seen him again. She had arranged a room swap with a finalist who wanted to live in college for the last weeks and taken the girl's digs at the far side of town. At the end of term she had steeled herself and gone up to Ash's room one last time to say goodbye. But he was already gone. He had, however, left a note on his desk. It felt like a consolation prize. She had read it once then torn in up, leaving the pieces in the waste paper bin in the Lodge.

'Dear Isabella,

I am more sorry than you know for the way it ended between us. Perhaps one day when I am older and wiser you might give me the chance to explain it all to you better. For now I can only ask that you will forgive me. I am sure that we shall meet again, if not in this life, then in the next, for I always felt I knew you from somewhere else, from somewhere before.

Remember this, twenty-five years from when we first met, I will wait for you in the Lodge. The first Sunday in October 2020 at 11 o'clock. I have no idea where or what we will be then. It will be twenty-five years since we first went up to Oxford, twenty-five years since matriculation. Promise me you will come.'

Now in her husband's study Isabella screwed up her eyes. After all these years she was not even sure if she remembered it right. First Sunday in October 2020 at 11 o'clock. Did Ash really write that note? And even if he had done, wherever he was in the world, he would have forgotten by now. And even if he did remember she was not sure that she wanted to know. Maybe she was just remembering things the way she wanted them to be. Perhaps the letter was a figment of her imagination muddied through time, a delusion born of the long exhausting years when the twins were babies and she had nightmares about drowning slowly in nappies and laundry. The night feeds, the endless illnesses that came like plagues, Jamie with his gluten allergy that for years went undiagnosed, and the tyranny of the bath time and bedtime story. The dictates of meal times, gluten free, and emptying the dishwasher, that had driven her to the brink of insanity and Tony into working ever longer hours. God knows she loved the twins more than her life. But motherhood had been a con as far as she was concerned, at least in the early years until the boys had gone to school. Even today, whenever she saw women in their uniform yummy Mummy navy striped T-shirts coo-ing over babies in prams, she wanted to hit them around the head with their chintz pattered nappy bags, to bring them to their senses. It was all a grand delusion. Going to Art College, part-time at first, had been her salvation. Without it, one of those days, she would have taken the long kitchen knife and slit her own throat. Ash had been right. She had been young and naïve, a Cinderella who could not think beyond the end of the fairy story and believed that love would be enough. But she understood now that it could get worn out, used up with long years of drudgery and routine.

And yet and yet. For years she had tried to convince herself that the prospect of an arranged marriage was the source of Ash's bouts of melancholic preoccupation at Oxford. A simple answer in retrospect. But she had known all along that the arranged marriage was not the cause. In truth she had never got to the bottom of it, never really understood him. Perhaps it was better it had ended the way it did after all?

The summer afterwards Isabella had requested a year out and gone to France. When she returned to Oxford the following year, he had already graduated. Is that why Joanna and the others had never mentioned Ash Misra, to protect her because they must have met his wife?

Isabella wiped the last of her tears with the back of her hand and put the photograph back into the album. She was a foolish, self-indulgent middle-aged woman! She was tired. Deep down she feared the two parts of her personality. There was the sensible rational self that managed and organised, ran a growing business and had not done such a bad job bringing up the twins. They were turning into fine young men. Then there was the other self, the one that was still looking for something, that cried out when she was alone at night. Where are you? Can you hear me?

Putting the albums away, she closed the cupboard firmly. Her legs were numb with pins and needles and she felt sick. Rubbing her calves to encourage the circulation of blood, she stood up and hobbled back to the computer desk. It occurred to her that she might search for Ash on Google but she decided not to waste time on it and clicked shut down. Taking the wine glass and bottle, she cast a quick eye round making sure everything was tidy just as Tony had left it. If the smallest thing were out of place, he would complain. From the landing she shouted to the boys to think about getting showered, then went into the bathroom and threw the remains of the wine from her glass down the toilet. However hard I try, she thought, I can never escape it. For she knew, as she always had, that if it had not been for Ash Misra, she would never have married Tony.

Chapter Six

Oxfordshire, Early October 2010

It was a cartoon road, grey with square banks and trees of green, rolling ahead into China blue. Even Isabella, with her artist's eye, could add no more diversity of colour to the day than that. It was a new road, a straight road, built to take you quickly from A to B with no need to meander through old villages and scenic spots. The only interests were the roundabouts and signposts that hinted at other stories that might be told; Juniper Hill, Silverstone, Stowe Gardens. But there was never any time.

To keep herself alert at the wheel, Isabella reached to the dashboard for a mint, biting it from the top of the packet. Changing down a gear she ceded passage to a silver Mercedes. A large red and black freight lorry stormed the outside lane of the roundabout from behind. She swerved inwards to the left, hitting the horn, narrowly avoiding the rear axle, swearing vociferously in Spanish, a legacy from her mother. The phone in her handbag on the passenger seat sounded the opening chords of Eric Clapton's *Layla*. Tony had set her ring tone last Boxing Day afternoon when reminiscing about songs of his youth with the boys.

Turning off the A43, she pulled up next to the entrance to a field road. The phone pinged with a text. She sighed at the inevitable, knowing it would be Tony or one of the boys. She was the centre of it all, chief operations officer, sorting, managing, fixing. Without her the family would fall apart.

'Is Dad coming for the rugby or not? It's nearly kick off.' It was Jamie.

No surprise there, she thought. Despite his obsessive attention to detail, Tony was unfailingly late. Late for nativity plays, harvest festivals school concerts, parents' evenings and rugby matches. So much so that no one asked them to dinner parties anymore.

'Should be on his way. U know Dad! Luv you.'

She hit send and switched off the phone. She could do no more. They were big enough to sort themselves out.

With her yellow tote handbag open on her lap Isabella stared across the fields. Flocks of crows circled and dived, gleaning the husks of wheat left by the combine harvesters. Pulling out her makeup case she flipped down the sunshade for the mirror.

Did she look alright? For once she was out of the studio and had made an effort. Pursing her lips she applied a soft coral red lipstick. Noting the small lines round her lips, she tilted the mirror and ran a brush through her hair. It was still fine and golden with only a few bits of grey. She had let it grow out of its six weekly crop into a layered shoulder length bob so it curled around her face.

Why was she doing this? Going back? Opening the Pandora's box? It was madness.

'The first Sunday, 11 o'clock, twenty-five years from now.' Damn it! The whole thing was insane.

The gates at Joanna and Gus's small country estate, Farndon, looked like they ought to have at least a pineapple if not a winged gryphon on the stone posts. Remiss of Joanna, not to buy a pair, Tony had always said. But the entrance was deliberately understated, hidden away off an unmade lane on a hill above an Oxfordshire village. It was a place reserved for people in the know. Built for carriages, the angle of the gate was such that visitors had to get out of their cars to ring the intercom. Blackberries grew wild up the red stone wall and a bee sat on the buzzer. Gently, Isabella pushed it away with the back of her hand. But it was late in the season and it fell dead into the nettles below.

'Hello. It's Isabella Harrington for lunch.' The gates clicked and opened, inviting her in.

Winding down the window, she set the car into first then second gear, rolling it gently down the drive that ran in a long arc from the top of the hill. The still warm air welcomed her like the loving palms of a parent, one on each cheek. She let the breeze play with her hair, anticipating the clearing in the trees to the right which would open the first of a series of vistas of the countryside below. Already she was losing a sense of reality and knew that she would be playing a role that would not be a comfortable one. It happened every time she came to Farndon where she was seduced and stifled at the same time. She had come more often when the twins were for small, for respite and friendship. Joanna and Gus had no children of their own but were nothing if not generous. There had been the summer weekends after Joanna was first elected when Parliament was in recess. The little boys had fished in the pond and swum naked in the swimming pool. She and Joanna had chatted and eaten a cream tea on the lawn. Those were the days when MPs were not afraid to gossip to friends. Suddenly for no reason,

Isabella remembered the shapes of the twins' heads when they were babies. Warm in her hands, she could tell them apart by touch alone. Ferdie's head was brick square, Jamie's rounder with a bump to the back right. Oh, and their tiny grasping hands and bare feet with toes like little pearls! At bath time she had been afraid she might snap them off by accident. At Farndon it had been a relief not to have to cook a meal and to let Joanna and Gus's staff take the domestic strain for a night or two. When was the last time she was here? Isabella struggled to recall. Lives had moved on and gobbled up the years. It had been a late autumn, when the leaves had been raked into great piles for bonfires. The men had gone off early to shoot, taking the excited twins with them. There had been shouts of 'hurry up,' 'wouldn't want to miss the show,' and much clattering and banging of guns and woollen stocking feet up and down the uncarpeted back stairs. Avoiding the morning shoot, Isabella had gone foraging for mushrooms in the woods and driven up in the Land Rover for beef broth and sausages between drives. In the afternoon she had stood behind the guns and reloaded. Jamie had hit a pheasant with a lady's gun and been blooded for the first time.

Sighing, she slowed the car. The morning mists had disappeared and the Buckinghamshire countryside rolled out like a great Persian carpet. In the distance the weathervane on the top of a church spire glinted gold.

Ahead and on the top of a small hill was the grand Georgian house, white painted with large windows and shiny black painted lintels, all in perfect proportion. The front door was wide open at the top of the semi-circular steps. Men had always gone out from here, up to London to Parliament, to the City, to fight great wars or to administer the British Empire. The scene suggested pride and entitlement and was as it had always been and supposed it was always meant to be, she thought; English and run from the Home Counties. Farndon was like that and it would be so easy to fall for it.

'Hello there!' Gus was coming out of the garages to the left, waving a chamois leather to flag her down. He continued to flap it somewhat irritatingly, standing behind the car as she reversed into a parking space.

'What a lovely day!' Isabella chipped perkily. In the distance a tractor ground away.

'Welcome! You look great, as always!' They kissed each other twice, once on each cheek.

'What's this? Chitty Chitty Bang Bang?' Isabella pointed at a green and silver classic racing car in the garage

'Come and see my new toy!' Gus flapped the chamois leather yet again, this time by way of invitation. The tail of his pink candy-striped Ralph Lauren shirt hung loosely at the back of his trousers and he had removed his cuff links and rolled up his sleeves. Isabella was shocked. It was at least three years since she had last visited Farndon and Gus was now looking his age. He was completely bald and walked with a slight stoop. She struggled to picture the dashing forty five year old divorced businessman Joanna had married when she was just twenty-five.

'A 1929 Bentley Blower. Isn't she beautiful?' Casually, Gus polished the bonnet and the huge headlights. Apparently, only fifty five were made originally. This one had the super- charger added in the nineteen thirties.' He indicated the unit fitted on the front of the car by the grill.

'I bought it from a chap in Nottingham, a distant relative of Tim Birkin, one of the original Bentley Boys. Get in!'

'It's like a Spitfire cockpit!' Isabella ran her hand over the dashes and dials on the board. Already she was keeping up appearances, playing her part.

'You can keep all your modern electronic wizardry! This is style! I am going to race her next year. Last chance saloon today though! I'm mothballing her for the winter after this weekend. You can take her for a spin round the park later if you like. I've had the pedals put back to the original; brake on the right, clutch on the left, accelerator in the middle. Go on, try!' Gingerly, Isabella touched the pedals with the tip of her toe. 'You'll soon get used to it!' Gus wiped his brow and looked straight ahead at the view.

'How are Tony and the boys? Must be getting big? But he gave her no time to answer. 'Thank you for coming. It means a lot to us both.'

'Of course I would come.' Isabella too looked at the view and saw a great bank of grey clouds to the west. 'Is there any news?'

'There is unlikely to be a criminal prosecution thank God, but her career's on the line. She's getting no help from the Party high ups. They want to satisfy the baying mob and win the next general election. There's no loyalty when it comes to this sort of thing. Gus sucked on his teeth, which Isabella knew were no longer all his own since Jamie had offered Uncle Gus a toffee.

'Not for me little man!' he had said. 'False teeth! Got them knocked out one too many times with a polo mallet.'

'At the very least I think Joanna will be suspended from the Party. I'm trying to persuade her to step down but she is having none of it. I didn't want her to stand at the last election; tried to talk her out of it.'

'Politics is her life. It always has been.'

They got out of the car. Isabella straightened her skirt and Gus went to the sink in the back of the garage to wash his hands. His jeans were too long and the hems frayed from dragging on the floor. The plumbing thumped a little and a gush of water splattered into the metal sink. His back was to her when he spoke.

'I love her, you know. I always have.'

'Of course you do!'

'I know people say she only married me for my money and because I could support her political career. Perhaps if we had had children…'

He turned, rolling his sleeves down and fastening the cuff links. He struggled with the right hand one and she reached out to help. He shrugged rolling his wrist upwards and grinning like a boy, then he tucked in his shirt.

'Come on! Into the lion's den! It's the usual suspects,' and yet it was as if he had pulled a visor down over his face.

The people in the conservatory on the east side of the house lolled and sprawled over settees. The scene reminded Isabella of an illustration of Jonah in a children's story book. It was as if they had all been swallowed into the stomach of a great whale and were awaiting their fate. Clutching at their champagne glasses, they eyed the far end of the room where the French windows had been left open, presenting an ocean of lawn. A few of the lucky guests had already been spewed out into the day.

Gus had disappeared but Anwar was there, as he was every time she came to Farndon, this time offering her drinks.

'Hello Miss Isabella. Champagne?'

'Anwar, how are you?' She was in a room full of old people, and she did not recognise any of them. It was easier to talk to the servant until she gathered her wits.

'Very well, thank you. Ferdie and Jamie are getting big now?'

'Yes, they will be fifteen in the summer.' Isabella smiled and moved on so he could serve the next guest.

Joanna was on the far side of the room, towering head and shoulders over everyone else. She nodded and waved as if to say, 'I'll get to you soon.' Nervously smoothing her skirt again, Isabella gingerly sipped her champagne. The focus of her mind adjusted like an old fashioned camera lens, in and out, nearly there. Familiar faces emerged from the ageing crowd, young people she had once known, presented now in the bodies of their parents perhaps? The men's jowls and beer bellies sagged in inverse proportion to the tight nipped, botox pumped face of their wives. With their immaculate blond highlighted hair, platinum and diamond rings and lipstick thick on thinning lips, Isabella knew them and yet she did not. Once again she smoothed her skirt. How did the dress code for these 'little' parties emerge? Clearly, she had got it wrong. She was wearing a cream-coloured skirt and blouse with a long brown silk cardigan, kitten heels and tiny pearl drop earrings. The ladies' code of the day was a wrap dress, preferably in blue, or grey, with incredibly high heels. With Gus as the only exception, the men all wore chinos with blue shirts and blazers.

'Isabella! It's Alex! You haven't changed!' A huge, red faced man suavely decorated with a yellow silk cravat, threw his arms out wide, and strode across the room. Isabella managed to deflect the bear hug into half an embrace by presenting a cheek and a right shoulder. For a second the room froze. Everyone looked, the women peering down their noses, their pinched makeup plastered faces turned to one side like beady eyed crows. Isabella was surprised for she had not seen Alex since the twins were small and they had never been close, but now she appeared to be his new best friend.

'So how are you? Joanna says you're painting! Must let me see some of your work! Actually, the wifey buys the art. There she is, over there.' With a careful jerk of his champagne glass, he indicated a younger woman with a neat black bob on the far side of the room. Already the woman was summing her up, running the checklist; age, figure, dress, threat level for this older woman whose friendship predated her own relationship with her husband. Thankfully at that moment, Joanna arrived

'Alex, Isabella! Wonderful to see you!' Kiss, kiss. The wonderful came out as an exaggerated 'wanderful.' Her voice had not changed, deep and considered, almost manly. Subtly branded in Berkshire and Cheltenham Ladies, it promised, I am one of us, trust me, I am born to lead. And it had served Joanna well in the House of Commons, until recently at least. Isabella pulled back from the empty embrace. She could not but notice Joanna's already large feet, generously augmented by a pair of turquoise and silver pointy-toed Moroccan style slippers. They might have belonged to a pantomime dame in Aladdin. This true blue Tory had always had a Bohemian streak. Typical Joanna! How reassuring! She too was immune to the dress code, even at her own parties, today bursting out of an autumn country style blouse printed with a pattern of ducks and a long denim skirt.

'Image consultant! Bah humbug!' She had once confided to

Isabella that her constituency party had employed one prior to a general election. 'I'm in politics because I believe in the issues, not to be a fashion model!'

'Isa, you look great! Joanna pronounced. 'All these upcoming exhibitions are clearly doing you the world of good!' It is far easier to pass judgement on others than on oneself, Isabella thought. But Joanna looked stressed. Her hair had grown out of its fringeless platinum blond bob and she had defaulted to pinning it on the top of her head. She had worn it like that when she was young but now the style was harsh and unflattering around her puffy powdered cheeks.

'Did you see Alex on *Question Time* last week? Made an excellent case for *British Energy*. And Alex, you absolutely must go and see Isabella's next exhibition! She paints the most wonderful abstract landscapes, full of colour. We've got a stunning piece on the landing. Go and see it after lunch! When is it again, your exhibition?'

'Small showing in Yorkshire in a few weeks, then the big one in New York in the spring.'

The words New York worked like a magic charm. Joanna's eyes widened and Alex was definitely paying attention.

'Wow, that's great,' he said.

'Tony certainly won't like you gallivanting off to the States. He wants you out of harm's way, safely up north at home, always has.' As ever Joanna's opinions were perfectly timed and not usually far off the mark. She waited a few practised seconds to let her salvo sink in before switching tack. 'Love your blouse Isabella? Where is it from?

'Marks and Spencer's,' Isabella lied on principle.

That foxed Joanna. She did not do jokes.

'All the old crowd here, Joanna.' Alex surveyed the assembled clan.

Surprise on the way though! You will never guess who I ran into in the Treasury last week!' Joanna's eyes danced with the joy of conspiracy and Isabella's heart sank. But Anwar was discreetly beckoning his mistress from the door and the next instant, Joanna was gone. Some things never changed. As always Joanna was jumping to it, off to answer some higher invisible call, going to meet, lobby and persuade. It had been the same when they were students. Isabella remembered her banging vigorously on College doors, dragging people out of bed, refusing to take no for an answer.

'Come on darling, help me. I've got to get out the vote. Isa, please?' And Isabella would acquiesce. She could not have given a fig about student politics, but her friend had always been important to her.

With Joanna gone, Alex's hand fluttered against the small of Isabella's back. Men often did that to her, perhaps because she was small and they perceived her to be fragile. But secretly, she wished that Tony would reach out and touch her in the same way, just once in a while.

'Look there!' he said pointing out a chap on the far side of the room. 'Between us, Will Gregory was pissed as hell about getting left out of the cabinet. Coalition government and all. Not enough seats for all the loyal bums. Like the Oxford Union all over again when they were cobbling together a government last May. I strolled down to Whitehall to see for myself. Plus ça change!' He downed the rest of his champagne in one, and parked his glass on top of the piano. 'God, I need some air! Shall we get out of here?'

Standing on the edge of the lawn in front of the house, they sighed with relief and giggled awkwardly at themselves. In the distance the tractor pressed on, desperately trying to outrun an advancing bank of clouds which rolled black, charcoal and grey, like great balls of wool across the valley floor.

Alex lit a cigarette, offering Isabella one from the packet. She shook her head.

'Never could give up. Miranda spent God knows how much on new curtains for the house last year and now I'm like a schoolboy again, exiled to the garden to smoke behind the wheelie bins.' He inhaled deeply and they watched the tractor slowly being swallowed up by the clouds.

'One had to turn out today and support. Bad form not to show up, under the circumstances.' He exhaled, the smoke fleeing on the breeze, as if to meet up with the advancing clouds.

'It will be such a shame if Joanna goes down like this. Perhaps the Crown Prosecution Service won't prosecute after all. Seems to me she is on a sticky wicket though, both with the Party and the Crown Prosecution Service.'

'I don't know what she will do without politics. It's her life.' Isabella said, not for the first time that day.

'I hadn't thought of it like that. Bloody Gus has invited me to play golf next week. He only does that when he wants something. My money is on him asking for a non-Exec position for Joanna. But I can't tell him I am on my way out too. I've done every job in the whole business. There isn't that much more I can do. DM Middle East, GM Asia, DIT Europe, HGO SA.'

Isabella raised an eyebrow but he continued to recite his acronymic curriculum vitae. The younger Alex would have seen the joke.

'I am on the board, but I'm not naïve enough to see that my days are not numbered. Trouble is one gets too expensive to employ and the young ones are pushing from underneath, hungry, sharp, keen like we used to be. I don't mind telling you I am looking around.' Another exhalation of cigarette smoke and he looked Isabella straight in the eye.

'You still married to Tony?'

'Yup. He is just back from Beijing. A little jet lagged this weekend. He sends his apologies'

'You're lucky. He's a nice steady chap. Miranda is my second wife, you know. You remember Jill?'

Of course Isabella remembered, for Jill was the girl she had swapped rooms with after splitting up with Ash.

'No marriage is ever perfect, and anyone who tells you otherwise is lying,' she commiserated. 'It's always an illusion, an ideal, a compromise, and damn hard work. Everyone does their best.' Isabella shivered. The wind was getting up. Normally she kept her own counsel, all her thoughts and emotions going into her painting. She was surprised to hear herself talk like this, piqued perhaps by Jo's remark about Tony keeping her at home. She remembered his face when she had told him about New York. It was a kind of bitter insouciance, and it had occurred to her that he was jealous because she might just be doing better than he was.

'I could always trust you, Isabella. You were different from the rest of us.' Alex confessed.

'I grew up abroad.' Isabella said. 'I wasn't interested in Westminster politics and merchant banking. I never really fitted in with all this, you know the London, the Home Counties set.' She gestured vaguely at the house and gardens.

He sighed, brooded a few seconds then changed the subject. 'We men are fools. We sell our souls to the highest bidder for ever increasing salaries and bonuses, sacrifice our first marriages and relationships with our children. At forty-five we get cut off at the knees with a chainsaw by the bank or business. Then what do we do? Rush off and marry a bright young thing who will copiously massage our ego, but who turns out to be just like our own wives twenty years ago, desperate for babies.' Dropping his cigarette butt on the lawn, he watched it glow for a few seconds, before tenderly stubbing it out with the tip of his shoe. 'And we end up paying for interior designers to hand paint smiley red and green dinosaurs on the nursery walls at the same time as paying university fees for the children of our first marriage. And the stupid thing is we pretend that the lady loves us, not the capital we have worked like hell to build up.'

'In our house the cute smiley dinosaurs have been replaced by real live grunting teenage ones.' Isabella attempted levity, but Alex was not to be distracted.

'Miranda doesn't really get me. Not really. We're the wrong generation and she has no comprehension of how I started out. Jill and I had a lot of shared history and, bugger me, I threw it all away.' He winced slightly at his own words. 'Still, could be worse. I could be on wife number three like our novelist friend over there, Felix Thomas.' He jutted his chin in the direction of a thin bald man who had his back to them by the French windows. 'Have you noticed? Every time he remarries, a new novel follows! Acquisition number three is Russian. I'd bet my bottom dollar right now he is writing a modern day Doctor Zhivago!'

A London taxi was purring down the drive. Isabella swallowed hard to quash a rising sense of panic. The taxi delivered a tall dark haired man to the front of the house. Oh God! What if it were Ash? Alex craned his neck as be bent down to pick up his cigarette butt, then stood up and wrapped it in a piece of tissue before depositing in his blazer pocket.

'Here comes our surprise! But I can't for the life of me see who it is. Can you?'

A long table had been placed in the hall to accommodate the guests who were too numerous for the dining room. Joanna and Gus held court from the heads of the table and Isabella found herself sandwiched between Felix Thomas and the surprise guest. He had turned out to be none other than the Chinaman, Li Bin. Isabella was dizzy with relief or was it disappointment? She was not sure.

'How amazing it was to bump into Joanna in Whitehall last week and get invited to her beautiful house. And now I find you all here twenty-five years from matriculation! That is real *yuan fen*. It means destiny, fate!'

'Cheers! To us!' Excitedly, Li Bin raised his wine glass to Felix and Isabella.

'I recognised Joanna immediately amongst the MPs, but she did not know me at first!' He chuckled patting his plump belly and gently slapping his own pudgy cheeks. Isabella was not surprised. Gone was the lanky, quiet young man with thick lenses and heavy rimmed 1950 style spectacles, who wore the same blue padded Mao jacket, seemingly all year in Oxford, regardless of the temperature. Li Bin had metamorphosed into a sophisticated, overfed business executive in a well-cut navy blazer.

At the far end of the hall the front door had been left wide open to let in fresh air. Isabella was glad of it. A shaft of sunlight fell onto the marble floor, but already the black clouds were blotting out the distant green. Abdul placed a starter in front of Isabella; a small filo quiche with red onions and a couple of pieces of asparagus on the side. Lunch was late and the guests, hungry past politeness, tucked in as soon as they were served.

'I work for China Invest.' Li Bin pronged his quiche, apparently without realising that he was the one that had caused the delay to lunch. 'We're interested in investing in London. Infrastructure.' He chuckled again. They laughed in response not entirely sure why then fell into the awkward silence as between people who might once have been called friends but who now realised they had always been strangers. There was no carpet in the hall and the din of voices made conversation hard work. Isabella had drunk too much. The faces of the people swelled and distended into a crazy menagerie; goats, horses, pigs and toads with their noses in the trough, croaking, honking, braying, all trying to outdo one another. Was it transmitted genetically, this precocious cocktail of establishment boorishness, poise and confidence that might be wrong but never entertained failure or doubt? Tony was part of it and she had done her best to belong to his world. It was what she thought she had wanted, but she had struggled. Her parents-in-law had always been critical. She had overheard the whispering on her wedding day.

'So who is this Isabella Angus? Are they the Anguses of Argyll?' Disapproving shakes of heads. 'Father a civil engineer or some such thing. Never heard of them.'

Now here at Farndon snippets of conversation flew around

the room. It was everyone for himself, catch one and ride it for as long as you could.

'Scandalous! My brother knows that deal.'

'No reason to work the poor boy like that.'

'They do it because they get away with it.'

'If you have not been to Africa, you have not lived!'

'Only one missing is that Indian chap-Misra.'

'You two still in touch?' Felix grinned cheekily at Isabella. Her stomach tightened

'No.' She tried to sound nonchalant, biting down on a red onion. It was bitter sweet with cheese and glaze.

'I'll never forget Old Mizzers! He cleaned my wounds and strapped me up one day. I was coming back from Wapping-remember the printers' dispute?' The aside was meant for Li Bin. 'I'd had an encounter with a truncheon and a hoof of a police horse. Mizzers spots me getting off the bus and coming up the High Street all bloodied, nursing my head.

'What the dickens?' he said and that made me laugh so much I threw up. He took me back to College and helped me clean up. I had always thought he was a bit of a wally until then. Funny thing, I'll always remember, he tut tutted, waggled his head in an exaggerated way and said, 'I thought you Britishers were supposed to be the civilized ones, our colonial masters and all that. I have come here for a bit of peace and quiet. But you lot are just as barbaric as us bloody Indians.'

The cheese curdled in Isabella's mouth.

Anwar put plates with small racks of lamb in front of them, the top bones beautifully finished with white paper crowns. The vegetables were passed, followed by the gravy and the salt and pepper. Li Bin ate slowly, struggling with the lamb. Isabella had stopped drinking because she would have to drive into Oxford after the party and her head was still muggy. The sunlight had disappeared from the door and the party began to sag in the middle. The collapse was intangible but real. People had got what they came for and could not wait for it to be over. Some began to make advance excuses, wanting an early get away. But Li Bin was still enthusiastic with his memories and anecdotes. He turned to Felix.

'I remember the time you unfurled the banner of Nelson Mandela in the main quad and also a banner of the great social-ist leader of the miners' strike, what was his name?'

'Arthur Scargill.' Isabella and Felix chimed in at once.

'Got me into the most awful trouble, that one!' Felix laughed and swigged his wine. 'Dear old Tarzan was in quite a flap about it.' They giggled at the memory of Sir Peter Roberts, Master of the College. He had had a long silver fringe in the style of the politician Michael Heseltine nicknamed Tarzan. 'He threatened to send me and half the Oxford University Labour Party down for it. And now look! Nelson is the darling of the world establishment and yours truly is apparently a 'gem' of the British literary establishment, according to *The Times* literary critic at any rate, and we, we are all here at Farndon! Felix choked a little on the wine at his own joke and Li Bin hid the remains of his lamb under some cabbage and carrots.

'These things come around!' the Li Bin said. 'Did I ever tell you that I used to be a red guard! Quite a rebel I was, when I was young, causing trouble, beating people up and smashing the four olds. Now look at me! I'm a little bourgeois capitalist roadster come to take my revenge for the Chinese Century of Humiliation. I'm here to exploit you English blood stinking imperialists! The white man has been in charge for far too long. Now it's time for the Chinese to be top dogs! Gan bei, cheers.' He grinned mischievously and raised his glass. But Isabella noted the glint in his eye and wasn't convinced it was meant as a joke.

After lunch the ladies took coffee in the conservatory. The wind rattled the single glazed, Edwardian fly windows. They had been left open and the first drops of rain pitter pattered lightly on the roof, falling lightly on the white tiled floor below. As Anwar circulated with the coffee pot the phalanx of clouds raced the final yards up the long lawn to engulf them.

'Rum truffle?' Joanna passed the plate around. 'Do try! Jamie, my godson, made them for me because they are my favourite. They're his speciality and gluten free.'

The guests murmured their appreciation and the wind began to clatter and howl around the ill-fitting windows in their aged steel frames. In the distance something fell with a loud bang, as overhead clouds passed like a giant spaceship blotting out the day. The rain poured in now through the open windows splattering the ladies below who grabbed their coffee cups and start to move towards the grand front door. Anwar abandoned his post and with Gus shouldered the heavy wooden window poles in an attempt to save the day. Faster and faster, louder and louder the rain drummed on the glass roof until it formed a single note and conversation was impossible.

'Let's adjourn to the sitting room!' Gus shouted, waving the ladies out into the hall. But it was too late; the party was over. The rats were leaving the sinking ship.

'It's been lovely! But we really must go.'

At the bottom of the stairs, Alex's wife Miranda lisped into her Blackberry to her nanny.

'Did you take her temperature? Have you given her Calpol? Okay, okay. We are leaving now.'

'Where's Joanna?' Alex asked. 'We can't leave without saying goodbye.'

'She'll be back soon,' Gus was valiantly trying to hold the line. 'The Chief Whip is on the phone. Please don't go. The rain will pass and we can take the Blower for a spin.'

Isabella sneaked off across the hall to the lavatory. The chairs around the lunch table remained where they had been left, all at different angles, some still facing the table, another two leg to leg up like an amorous couple. Already the staff was clearing up, tipping the cutlery into a red plastic washing up bowl and stacking the plates. Isabella stopped to pick up a napkin from the floor, folded it and put it back on the table. Years of living with Tony must have rubbed off, she thought.

When she got back to the lobby the exodus was in full swing. *Give Joanna my love, if there is anything we can do?* Kisses, handshakes, hushed tones; the party had become a wake. Li Bin hitched a lift with some guests and their car looped ceremoniously round the turning circle as he waved regally through the windows to Gus. Anwar escorted others in turn to their cars under a giant Lord's umbrella and soon Isa's companions were down to three; Joanna, Gus and the red haired Will Gregory MP, standing limply on the cold stone steps. Almost as soon as they had come the clouds were clearing in the east, presenting distant stripes of baby blue, as the rain softened into a gentle shower.

'I really ought to be going soon too, Gus.' Isabella knew

from bitter experience that if you waited for Joanna you would wait for hours. If she stayed it could be the early hours before she got away.

'It's OK Isa, I understand.' The fight had gone out of Gus. 'You need to get back. The boys will be waiting.'

She did not correct him.

'I'll stay, don't worry.' Felix volunteered, somewhat out of character for him.

Gus managed half a smile. 'Thank you.'

Isabella nodded with pursed lips and turned to kiss Gus.

'I can come back anytime, if you need me. Just let me know. Give Joanna a big hug from me.'

He nodded, grey, tired and old.

'No! Don't take me to the car, I can manage.'

She ran across the forecourt and down the drive, skirting and skipping the puddles, gulping the fresh air, catching the rain in her mouth, letting it soak her hair, her blouse, her chest, and did not give a damn.

Chapter Eight

Oxford, Early October 2010

It was unexpectedly chilly in Isabella's room in the Rexeter Hotel in Oxford. She fiddled with the radiator knob but, encrusted by paint and time, it would not budge. Giving up, she heaved up the old sash window to let in some air. Blue and green bins were lined up like sentries three storeys below and the rain drizzled from the pewter sky into the spaces between the buildings. A lead gutter had come away from the wall and the remains of the earlier downpour gushed from the top corner of the building to Isabella's left. It must have been like that a long time for the wall was stained green with wet moss. One storey below, wire net stretched across the space between the buildings. Was it to keep the birds out or to catch despairing guests who had made the pilgrimage to Oxford in search of dreams and found only disappointment and despair? Even the pigeons appeared to have abandoned the day as a bad job for there were none to be seen.

Turning from the window, Isabella went to unpack her over-night bag. The décor in the room was fake Oxford college; mahogany veneer furniture, bedspread and curtains with yellow stripes and blue trim and two small leather armchairs in far better condition than any in a junior common room Isabella had ever been in. The finishing touch hung proudly over the bed; a large black and white print of an unidentified eight rowing on the river. It was an Oxford experience invented by an interior designer in New England. Isabella was irritated but not by the packaging and franchising of the Oxford she remembered, but because she was not sure why she was there at all. She had been back only once before and that was to graduate in the autumn of 1989 with her ermine hood in the Latin ceremony at the Sheldonian Theatre.

Isabella pulled out her toilet bag, her striped cotton pyjama bottoms and a red vest top and put them all on the bed. Picking up the leather case containing the hotel information, she flicked the pages. There were advertisements for facials, hot stone massages, manicures and pedicures in the spa and high tea in the bar for £12.99 including Bucks fizz.

Why on earth had she come? It was irresponsible to disturb old memories and wake sleeping ghosts. She shuddered at the memory of her student time in France, how she had let herself be seduced by the fifty year old Director of the school where she had taught English. With his flabby stomach, tobacco breath, trendy blue and grey checked jackets, he had groped her breasts in his office at the end of her second week. His curly, grey, shoulder length hair might have been sexy if it had not been for the fact that he had gone bald on top, so that he looked rather like a hippy medieval monk. Without doubt he had been handsome as a young man but he still fancied himself as debonair. Isabella had never liked him much and had recognised him instantly as a rogue. But he had lusted after her young body, her pert nipples, narrow hips and flat belly. He had wanted her. She had given herself up, was wanton with him because it dulled the pain. A good Catholic, or so he said, he went to mass every Sunday with his crow faced wife and youngest child in tow. Isabella had stopped going to church after her mother died. She had finished the affair after a sordid Easter weekend in a cheap hotel in La Baule. The weather had been cold and wet, the sex bad and his wife had found out and left a message for Monsieur Le Director at reception. Afterwards, he had called Isabella an English whore so she had calmly arranged a transfer to a college far away in the south of France for her final semester. And then there had been the bleakness of her remaining student life in Oxford. Her memory of that time was like a grey rain lashed seascape. All her friends had graduated and she had lived as a hermit, not eating regularly, going to bed late and rising at noon until the days blurred into the night. She hid herself in the library at the Oxford Union or stayed in her room, always with her nose in her books. In the end, she had limped through finals on brandy, vitamin pills and prescription sleeping tablets and was astonished to emerge with a 2.1. On graduation, somehow or other she had got a job and moved to London. That's when Tony had come into her life. Good old Tony, kind, utterly predictable with his little routines, steady, completely unimaginative, hard-working and boring. He had taken care of her, given her stability. Isabella shook herself, forcing herself to concentrate on the pattern on the gold bedspread, counting the roses in threes until her mind settled. Brusquely, as if she were talking to her boys, she ordered herself to have an early night, read the Sunday papers in bed in the morning and then head home. There was no point going to College. Ash wouldn't show up and even if he did, she did not want to see him. There was no way she was going back to that dark, hopeless place.

A sudden shaft of sunlight caught her eye, cutting through the murk and disappearing again. She watched the swirling clouds, waiting for the sun to reappear. It might have been one or two minutes, until the dim yellow disc coaxed open the gaps between the clouds. But Isabella was ready with her sketch pad to catch the angle of the streaming strands of gold as they fell through the window, scattering tiny rainbow butterflies from the chandelier onto the carpet at her feet.

It was later than she thought when she left the hotel, getting on for five o'clock. The sun had worked quickly to clear the grey, leaving a clear blue sky and an invigorating freshness. She did not know where she was going and when it came to this, could never help herself. The family called it 'chasing the light.' There were times when she abandoned everything and headed out with her sketch book to capture the tiny moments when the colours changed and the shadows shifted. It was like that with every new piece of work. Something called and she answered. And her drawing would be marked all over with strange hieroglyphics that she had developed over the years; her own special code for marking the colours and mixes that came into her mind as she worked.

Isabella strolled through Gloucester Green where the café owners wiped the wet from the outside tables and the taxi drivers leant out of the windows of their cars. They gossiped in Urdu and her heart jumped. It was her lost baby language, the one Meena had given her. The sound of it, even the gruff uneducated banter of the taxi drivers suggested to her a story of love, warmth and comfort and a childhood that she had never truly had.

She wandered through the streets. Oxford was clinging on to the remains of summer, for an hour at least, for one last fling. The wet pavements glistened silver and the late afternoon shoppers tied their rain coats and jumpers round their waists and shoulders, folded their umbrellas and tarried in the sunshine. A band from Peru sang a gravelly, *Besame Mucho*.

Kiss Me, Kiss Me Lots,
As If It Were The Last Time.

A crowd had gathered to listen. Isabella stood at the back watching the sun drawing orange and black triangles across the wooden beamed Tudor façade of a shop. She sketched the plump children with ice cream round their mouths dropping pennies into the busker's purple cloth hat. Everything had changed since she was a student, the shop names, the hair styles and fashions, yet nothing had changed. The Saturday shoppers, the shadow of Christ Church Cathedral Tower falling over St. Aldates, and the shabby façade of Marks and Spencer's, all were still there.

She dodged a speeding bus splashing through a puddle. The light bounced off the shop windows creating multiple reflections on both sides of the glass. Isabella had the impression of worlds of people flitting over time, layered one on top of another like slides in a projector. She stopped to look at a pair of cream high heeled patent shoes in a window. There appeared to be two pairs of shoes, the ones she saw, the real ones, and the other pair like a ghost picture hanging as a shadow in space just behind. She went in and tried them on, looking at herself in the long chrome framed mirror. The shoes had a hidden platform in the sole. They made her look tall and her legs very thin, perfect for the exhibition in New York. It was an impulse buy and they were expensive. Tony was right. She had needed to get out of the studio!

Swinging her bag and dancing a little to the beat of *Besame Mucho* in her head, she walked. On her left she passed the little restaurant with the wrought iron spiral staircase into the basement where she and Ash had once eaten pizza. The past returned now in snippets of music and sensation. *Vaishnav Jana*, Gandhi's favourite prayer sung by Ash's mother that he used to play on his battered cassette recorder, the smell of violin rosin, the ropey final orchestra rehearsals in cold college chapels. After Isabella had got back from Paris and Ash was not there, she had thrown herself into music, playing everything everywhere. The Mozart Requiem in Merton, Vivaldi in Queen's, Tchaikovsky in Keeble were the performances she remembered

In the Covered Market they were shutting up shop, banging down the shutters on the butchers, the bakers, the handbag and jumper shop. The place smelt of sawdust, suddenly chill, vaguely metallic of blood overlaid with a milky sweetness from *Millie's Cookies*. Outside this shop a group of Spanish tourists had gathered buying the last freshly baked chocolate chip cookies of the day.

At the bottom of the High, Isabella stood on Magdalen Bridge sketching the punts in the pond green shadows of the bank. Abruptly, she closed her book and turned back up the street. She was not thinking where she was going. She just followed.

Kiss me, Kiss me lots,
As If It Were The Last Time.

Her little heels tapped the rhythm of the rumba on the pavement. She returned the way she had always gone as a student.

It was a simple short cut back to College up a narrow lane.

When Isabella was a fresher, it had seemed a magical secret alley, only for the anointed ones, those in the know, a passage between the past and the present, from one part of her day to another, going down to a rehearsal or for a cheap Chinese in Cowley, coming back home to College for supper or to work in the library. It was Alex Baines who had first shown her the way. He had whizzed down the hill, his feet up on the handlebars of his baker boy bike singing at the top of his voice.

We are the champions of the world
We are the champions of the world

And now, twenty-five years later, the timeless lane swallowed her up with silence and age as it had done on that fateful winter's night all those years. It had been at the end of her first term in Oxford, not long before Christmas, when it had all started with Ash; the beginning before the end.

CHAPTER NINE

Oxford, December 1985

High windowless college walls flanked the young Isabella, her only company, the stars. The tyres of her bike hissed softly like sleepy snakes over the damp cobbles, her bike light a limp white. Despite two hours of violin rehearsal her hands were cold on the handlebars: she had forgotten her gloves. But warm with the music of Christmas, she did not feel the cold.

In the deep mid-winter frosty wind made moan,
Earth stood hard as iron, water like a stone.

She hummed, and her wheels whirred through the puddles spinning Catherine wheels of spurting silver in the dark. On the left, the shadows had gathered thick and impenetrable. Suddenly she was wary. It was too still, too quiet. Something was not right. Her heart thumped in her chest. She was not sure whether to pedal faster, to slow down, or turn around and go via the main road instead. Then she heard it. Repeated, muffled thumps, and the crash of a bike against a wall.

'Fucking bastard! That'll teach you!' one voice.

'Stop! Enough!' Another, a young man's voice, gruff and hoarse.

'You've fucking killed him.' A third voice, a groan and a sharp crack and another, like snapping sticks.

'Someone's coming. Quick! Let's go! Com'on!'

Isabella braked softly, quietly letting her bike come to a stop. Cowering in the shadows of the left hand wall just before the bend in the lane, she tried to think. The men were running quickly up the lane. She waited, her breath smoking into the freezing night in sharp puffs. Eventually, when all was silent, she inched forward to peek around the corner. In the light of the old lantern street light she saw a bike lying in the middle of the lane, a bag and a body huddled in the shadows.

Leaving her bike, cautiously she made an approach. A broad shouldered man lay with his knees up and face to the wall, his hands still around his head. Timidly, she bent down and touched him on the shoulder.

'Are you alright?' What a stupid thing to say. He was heavy and she could not move him. What to do? She tried again and he moaned turning his face towards her. Except there was no face to see for it was covered in blood. Yet in that instant she knew him. Ash Misra, the Indian with the ridiculous moustache who lived in the top rooms on her staircase. The man had not even known how to do his own laundry when he first arrived and he regularly disturbed her and Joanna crashing up and down the wooden staircase at all hours as he passed their doors. Other than that and the fact that he was a cricketer and that she had briefly chatted to him at drinks in Freshers' Week, she knew nothing about him.

'Angus,' he called her now by her surname in the public school way. Blinking hard he tried to wipe the blood out of his eyes with the back of his hand.

'Run, run. You have to get out of here. Run, run, run!' He grabbed her upper arm muttering some words urgently in Hindi. But the effort was too much and he faded back into semi-consciousness.

Isabella removed her violin strapped to her back and looked up and down the lane. Ash's kit bag lay abandoned next to his bike and she went over to open it. Rummaging through, cricket bat, helmet, she found what she was looking for, a small wet towel and water bottle. She shook it. It was half-full. For extra measure she grabbed the cricket bat, propping it against the wall next to Ash.

'Ash, Ash.' She tried to wipe the blood away from his face but it kept coming, pouring out of large gash on his left forehead and the corner of his mouth. He groaned again.

'No! Go! Go now!' He was tremendously agitated, pushing her away and she realised that he thought he was somewhere else. 'They'll kill you. Run! Run!' More incomprehensible Hindi.

'Ash it's alright. You are in Oxford with me. Someone has attacked you but they've gone away now.' She sounded a lot more confident than she felt.

'Oxford? Oxford? Oh yes.'

'Drink this?' She put the water bottle to his lips, or at least where she thought his mouth might be under his blood drenched-moustache.

'Good.'

The towel was already soaked with blood and still more came.

'I can't stop the bleeding.' Her voice was tight with panic and he put his hand on hers.

'Press hard. It will stop soon enough.' He raised his head for more water and she supported it with the back of her hand, easing it into her lap. The water gushed over his chin, wetting his clothes with streams of diluted blood. Cradling his head she reached over and managed to open her violin case taking out the cloth she used to wipe away the rosin dust. With it she tried to stem the flow. They sat in silence in the dark, waiting for the blood to stop.

Gingerly, she took her hand away from the makeshift compress.

'I think you've broken something. Perhaps you shouldn't move. I'll go to College and call an ambulance.'

'No! Help me sit up! I can walk.'

Gradually they managed sitting and then standing. Grimacing with pain and leaning against the wall to get his balance, Ash caught sight of the cricket bat.

'Bloody good thing those goons did not find that bat. They would have killed me! They were five of them, came out of nowhere, drunk as lords. Called me a fuckin' Paki. Told me to go back to where I came from.'

'Hush,' Isabella said. 'Not now.'

'Fuckin' Paki! It's so bloody funny. If only they knew!' He started to laugh almost hysterically but it was swallowed in a groan of pain.

They abandoned the bikes and cricket bag taking the violin and cricket bat which Ash used as a crutch. It was not far back to College but it seemed to take an age to get there. Ash leant increasingly heavily on Isabella to the point where she felt he would almost crush her. He rested briefly under the Bridge of Sighs leaning on the wall of a neighbouring college, coughing, spitting blood, gasping with pain. Their College beckoned, lit up like a Christmas card just further up the street. Lights streamed out of the windows and there was a large Christmas tree out front with red and green fairy lights and a gold star on top.

Ash was breathing unsteadily wheezing and gasping. Somehow they made it the last fifty yards and over the threshold into the Lodge.

'What on earth?' Taff the Welsh Head Porter with his terrifying white scarred face, looked up at them over the top of his half-moon spectacles.

'Mr Misra is that you Sir? Jimmy get out here!' He shouted to the junior porter and came out into the lobby.

'Ran into some thugs. Beat me up. Angus, Isabella found me.' Ash panted.

'Let's get you inside, Sir. You're going to have a bit of a headache in the morning.' Taff had been badly burned in the Falklands war and the damaged facial nerves and grafted skin had left him with a perpetual ghost like expression. But the emotion was to be found in his voice, a rich gentle Welsh accent reminiscent of Richard Burton that promised valleys of harp, song and poetry.

'Let him go Miss, please! It's alright. I've got him.' But Isabella would not give him up, for she did not want anyone else to hurt him. Strangely, Taff seemed to understand, coaxing her out from under Ash's arm, taking the weight himself.

'Jimmy, take Miss Angus into the Lodge and call an ambulance. I can manage. Sensing the strength of the other man, Isabella peeled away and at last Ash surrendered, letting himself slump heavily onto the stocky ex-Welsh Guard.

The tiny porters' room at the back of the Lodge smelled of coffee and cigarette smoke. They were engulfed by the warmth from the two bar electric fire in the corner next to the kettle and Taff's famous Italian coffee pot.

'Easy does it!' Taff helped Ash to sit in the big leather

armchair in the middle of the room. In the light Isabella saw for the first time the full extent of Ash's injuries. Already his face was swelling and distended, purple, red and black with bruises, cut and blood.

'Tut tut. Just you wait till I get my hands on the scum that did this to you.' Taff propped Ash up with a cushion. 'Let's undo your anorak a bit, Sir. Make you more comfortable.' Taff's right hand had lost all of the index finger and the top half of the rest of the fingers on his hand were streaked white and tight with burn marks. Ash reached to help, the brown hand and the deformed hand, battling for a moment, the zip stuck in blooded navy nylon.

'The ambulance is on its way, Sir.' Jimmy popped his head round the door. Isabella started to shake. Teeth chattering, suddenly cold, she fought back the tears. Looking down she saw that she too was covered in Ash's sticky wet blood. Her hands, her tartan jacket, and her jeans clotted with purple blobs and streaky red wheals.

'It's alright Miss. Just a bit of shock. Sit down.' Taff pulled out his desk chair for Isabella and handed her a packet of tissues, indicating with a gesture that she needed to wipe her face. 'Jimmy, make Miss Angus some tea with plenty of sugar!' She put her hand to her cheek and her hair. It was matted to the right hand side of her head with Ash's blood.

Then everything happened in a rush around her; Taff pulling out the first aid kit, the ambulance men in their green fatigues and big boots squeezing into the tiny room, and laying Ash on the stretcher which seemed far too narrow for him. She got up to go with him to the hospital.

'No Miss! Taff's hand was on her shoulder. You stay here.

Get some supper and rest. I'll go with him.' It was an order not a request. 'Don't worry! Looks far worse than it is. Come and see me in the morning!'

Taff had not been in the Lodge after breakfast but he had left Isabella a note in her pigeon hole.

All well. Patient resting.
See you at lunch time.
Don't worry!
Taff.

Reluctantly, Isabella went to lectures but was unable to concentrate on the lecturer's dry analysis of Racine's *Andromache*. She did an hour in the library trying to write an essay, but was irritated by the chatter of the lawyers, and was glad when it was time to go down for lunch.

Taff was waiting in the Lodge, his voice smiling and light even if he face was paralysed into a white scared grimace.

'You look a lot better this morning, Miss. Gave me a proper fright you two warriors did, limping in like that last night.'

'How is he?' She was breathless.

'Couple of broken ribs and a few stitches to the head. Nothing that won't heal. The Master has asked you to pop up for tea later this afternoon, any time after three. He went to the hospital himself this morning.'

'But I was thinking to go to myself, this afternoon to see Ash?' She protested. She would rather see Ash than Sir Peter, the old Master.

'Don't worry about Mr Misra. Let him sleep. He's a fighter that one. He'll be back soon enough.'

That afternoon, Isabella sat amongst the chintz roses on the sofa in Sir Peter's study, warming herself by the fire. Already it was dark outside and the grandfather clock marked stately time in the corner of the room.

'Terrible thing!' Sir Peter poured her tea and offered her a mince pie. He was a tall thin man with an energetic manner which belied nervousness. She thought it a strange trait for such an eminent retired diplomat. He talked slowly with gravitas, taking his time over the initial consonants so that Isabella wondered if he might once have had a stutter.

'How is Ash?' she asked again.

'In good spirits. Very concerned that he will make the Varsity cricket team this summer.' He grinned displaying a spark of youthful mischief. 'Such are the important things in life!'

'When will he be able to come home, to College, I mean?' She corrected herself.

'Yes. College is home for many of us Miss Angus.'

'They will keep him in another night for observation, just to be on the safe side. He has some concussion.'

'Then I shall go and visit. Which ward is he in?'

'Best leave it until tomorrow. I suspect they will discharge him by then anyway. The police interviewed him this morning when I was there and he is tired. Let him sleep tonight. I have suggested that he move to a guest room on the ground floor when he gets back so as to avoid having to climb the stairs.'

She bit into the mince pie. It was sweet and warm laced with brandy. Sir Peter leant forward to the coffee table to pick up his cup and saucer, then sat back wearily in the chair. Sighing, he sipped his tea, his eyelids dropping in a way that reminded Isabella of statues of the Buddha in meditation.

'I'm afraid the police also want to have a word with you, Miss Angus.' He went on. 'It would be a help, if you don't mind. Just tell them what you saw. From Mr Misra's testimony, it was a gratuitous racial attack.'

'I didn't see anything much. They'd gone by the time I arrived. But I heard voices.'

'Good. I will do everything I can to make sure there is a prosecution for this.' His eyes turned cold, grey and distant over the top of his teacup and there was a retreat in him, a subtle recoil like a snail pulling in its horns and shrinking back into its shell. There was more to 'Tarzan' than the kind buffoon of a Master who was the butt of student jokes. Isabella did not know exactly what it was but recognised something from her own experience; that stalking blackness that nips at the corners of the mind, tormenting with thoughts of what might have been. Oh Mum! What a waste. I'm so sorry. If only I could have done more. Made you happy, made it right.

'It was a brave thing you did last night, Miss Angus.' Sir Peter pushed his long grey mane back over his forehead with his hand.

'Anyone would have done the same thing.' Isabella fiddled with the handle of the teacup.

'No. Many would have walked by on the other side. I have seen a lot of life, too much I think. I am more angry and ashamed than you can imagine when I see this happen to one of our students, especially an Indian student, not fifty yards from the College gates. We ought to be better than this.' He pointed at the two mince pies left on the plate forcing a smile. 'Come on let's finish them up!'

The next afternoon Isabella hurried across the quad to her room. Dusk was falling bringing with it a few snowflakes. It was barely four o'clock. Already lights were on in the College chapel illuminating the stained glass windows. They presented glorious visions of the Virgin and Child and the saints in a mosaic of red, green, purple and gold. The big wooden chapel door had been left open and organ music boomed out into the night. It was the time when the organ scholars practised. The opening bars of Bach's D-minor Toccata and Fugue expanded the darkness, vibrating through the paving stones and soles of Isabella's feet, up into her chest, and for a moment, she thought, she could almost fly.

Ash was back but had refused Sir Peter's offer of a guest room preferring to battle the stairs and be back in his own room. This, Taff had told Isabella with an uncharacteristic mischievous twinkle in his eyes.

Diving into the bottom of their staircase, she clattered up the stairs as the Bach faded into the darkness behind her. She passed her own room and that of Joanna with its pencil and note pad stuck on the door and the usual long list of notes from visitors. Climbing another loop, she was soon at the top. She had never been up there before. Her heart thumped and she faltered, feeling shy. What was she going to say to this strange Indian man with the ridiculous moustache? Would he think her forward, mistake her intention in knocking on his door, when actually she was just being kind? Then she heard another type of music, a high pitched sweet woman's voice singing gently in Hindi to a tabla beat. Mesmerized, she tiptoed the last few steps stopping with her hand on the top banister to listen. The outer wooden door to Ash's room was open inviting visitors, and the music was a recording coming from within. Again she hesitated and was on the point of turning away.

'Isabella? Is that you?' Ash called from inside. There was no time to answer as he pushed open the oak. He was wearing tracksuit bottoms and T-shirt standing by the sink lathering a shaving brush in shaving cream.

'Well, come in!'

His room was small and tidy, the bed made with the blue blanket neatly turned down, the books and papers lined up on the desk.

'Do you want some fruit cake?' Sir Peter's wife sent it up.

'Oh the English and their faith in tea and cake! I'm so sorry about what happened. You come all this way to study and this happens. How are you? I've been worried.' She wished she hadn't added the last bit. She didn't want to mention that his face was swollen a glorious yellow and purple.

He laughed and shrugged his shoulders, indicating the bandage over his right forehead which made him look like a wounded cartoon teddy bear.

Now it was his turn to be shy. He dithered from one foot to the other and she smiled awkwardly, listening to the woman singing.

'It's a beautiful song. Very sad.'

'No, it's not sad. It's *Vaishava Jana To*, Gandhi's favourite prayer. This is my mother singing with my cousin playing tabla. They made a recording for me to bring to England.' He switched off the tape recorder.

'Well, I should go.' Isabella nodded at the shaving brush in his hand. 'If you need anything please let me know.'

He grinned. 'Now you are here, I need you to help me shave. This damn moustache has got to come off.'

'Heavens no! I don't know how to shave. You would be better doing it yourself. I might cut off your nose by mistake!'

'Are you refusing an invalid's request?' He had already pre-positioned the desk chair in front of the sink. Now he put a towel round his shoulders and slowly, with a grimace, lowered himself into it. 'Come on!'

'Are you sure? You don't have to shave just because you got beaten up.'

'Do you like it? The moustache?'

'Well, no, not really. It does look a bit like some Colonel Blimp and in our culture, well... ,' she frowned not wanting to offend him.

'A bit well what? Tell me!'

'It's rather out of fashion I suppose we consider it to be a tad untrustworthy. Perhaps because you can't see the whole face.'

'Exactly. I look like a real wally wallah!' He grinned widely in appreciation of his own word play. 'It has to come off.'

Isabella twisted her long hair several times and fixed it up in a bun on the back of her head with a band she kept on her wrist, then carefully lathered the top of his mouth, avoiding the worst of the cuts and bruises.

'Are you sure? It's going to sting like the devil.'

He nodded and like a child waiting to have his face washed, stuck out his chin and tipped back his head. Reluctantly she picked up the razor and gently, with the tips of her fingers, touched his face and made the first stroke downwards and to the right of his mouth. Again and again she drew the razor, scraping, scratching through the coarse black moustache, leaving pink track marks in the white mounds of foam, flicking the surplus foam into the sink. She felt his hot breath on her hand and the thump of her own heart. His big brown eyes never left her face and he winced only once when she pulled a little at the cut on his lip.

At last it was done and she rinsed the razor, washing the residue of soap and the tiny black hairs down the sink. Taking the towel, he wiped himself, stroked his top lip where his moustache had been and abruptly walked away. He stood in the middle of the room with his back to her, looking up at the window which was too high and dark to see out of.

'What's the matter? Don't you like it?'

He turned quickly, took a step towards her and drew her to him. Instinctively she put her arms around him, hiding her head into his chest. She had not sought it but now in the silence of his arms she found a place. She had been travelling all her life and suddenly without expectation for a little while at least, she had arrived.

'Ouch! My ribs!' He tried to laugh but she felt the energy drain out of him, and recognised the pallor of exhaustion that comes when painkillers fade.

Taking his hand, she led him to sit on the edge of the bed.

'Did they give you some painkillers?'

'Yes.' He pointed to a red packet of tablets on the chair next to the bed.

'When did you last take some?'

'This morning before I left the hospital. But I don't think they will do any good. Not for this. Not for what I've got.' He was suddenly naked, vulnerable, without his moustache, very young, gaunt and pale.

'Why not? They won't do you any harm. No point being a hero.'

Isabella got up, fetched a glass of water and read the instructions on the packe*t; two four times a day.*

'The thing about pain is that you have to keep on top of it. Take them and you will rest better and recover more quickly.' She had learnt that at the hospital in the last months of her mother's life.

He waved the tablets away, closing his eyes reaching to kiss her, softly, conscious of his own fragility, and this time she did not pull away.

'That's my God up there.' He pointed to a framed picture of Shiva in blue and gold, the only adornment in his room. 'Do you think it's rude to kiss in front of a God?'

'Under the circumstances, I think a God would understand.'

'Stay with me a while, Isabella.' He savoured her name, running her finger over his lips where his moustache had been. 'I don't want to be alone. Let's face it, I am hardly in a position to take advantage!' Cautiously, he lowered himself onto his side and adjusted the pillows behind his head and back. She went to close the outside door and came to sit on the edge of the bed next to him. Reaching up he pulled the bobble out of her hair, watching as it tumbled down her back.

'You are so beautiful. Like an angel descended from heaven.'

'Don't be ridiculous!' she laughed.

Tenderly he stroked the long tresses with his hand, gathering them and pulling them around the left side of her face where he twisted the hair around his index finger making curls, letting them slowly unravel again.

'I had a friend once,' he said. 'He too had beautiful hair, just like you. In our first year at boarding school I used to comb it for him. Can you believe, we were barely eleven when they sent us away? His hair was thicker than yours which is so fine like gold thread. His was jet black, went right down to his waist and sometimes he couldn't get the knots out.' Ash stopped, exhausted as if the effort of conversation was too much for him. And there was a distant look of age and a strange defeat that Isabella would only recognise in time.

A horn hooted in the road outside. She did not know what to say. She sensed a far off place with heat and noise and a woman singing, a world she knew little about. She put her palm on his chest, reassuring him, feeling it move as he talked.

'We were so little when they sent us away to school. Our noses barely over the tops of the sink in the bathroom, Shivraj and I. The other boys bullied him because his Dad was from the Punjab. And they had it in for me too at first because my Dad wasn't a civil service man or an army officer. They came for us both one night not long after we started at the school, dragged us into the showers and holding us under them. We fought like tigers, kicking, biting and scratching. At that age I was bigger and stronger and they gave up on me and turned to Shiv, grabbing him by the hair and shoving his face into the sink until I thought they would drown him. We cried in each other's arms that night, both of us missing our mothers, but not daring to say it. That was the first time I combed his hair. It was wet and tangled and I combed it out like I used to do with my sister. Shiv and I shared the same bed that night, arms round until the early morning when I sneaked back into my own bunk. After that we were inseparable, watching out for each other at meal times, in the toilets. But the cricket nets were our refuge. We were out there even in the heat when the big boys shunned it, for there we could see the bullies coming and also the masters could see us from their staff room. It was not long before we took our revenge, out on the field. It is funny to think about it now because at that age Shiv was smaller than I was but at that time he was the demon batsman, whacking the bullies for six after humiliating six, and I was the bowler cleaning up the wickets. Funny that!

Later, one summer, he had a growth spurt and came back over six foot tall, even taller with his turban on. No one messed with that Sardar anymore. Wah! He was so handsome. All the girls were in love with him! And by then we were well established on the cricket field. I was top of the batting order and Shiv, well Shiv! I wish you could have seen him bowl, all legs and arms, levers and speed and my, the stumps would fly right out of the ground!' Ash's arms shot up in demonstration but were hindered by bandages and pain. 'Beautiful! And the two of us thought we were the bee's knees! He was my brother, my best pal in all the world but in the end, in the end.' Ash's voice cracked.

'I let him down.'

'How so? I am sure it can't be like that?' Isabella reached up to draw the curtains over the window high above the bed.

Ash sighed.

'India is complicated. You cannot imagine how poor the people are, so many uneducated, ignorant and superstitious. They are easily whipped up into a mob, especially in Delhi which is a city of refugees, everyone fighting for air, space, water, a place to put down roots and start again. It is not a nice quiet place like Oxford or London. You have to eat the next man before he gobbles you up. It's like that.' Ash stared at the white door at the far end of the room, looking into a distant and terrible place.

'I am not sure that Oxford is a nice place after yesterday.' Isabella whispered.

But Ash had closed his eyes.

'I think I will have those painkillers now. Will you stay with me, just a cuddle, just a little while?'

CHAPTER 11

Oxford, early October 2010

A click of the switch and Sir Peter, former Master of Woodstock College, blinked as the kitchen neon stuttered white in the early morning haze. Foxy's paws scattered pattered across the linoleum and faded over the patio into the garden. Sir Peter was not sure about sounds anymore, whether he felt, heard or remembered them, or indeed whether they were within or without. But there was one sound in his life that was always there. Every morning when cooking breakfast and last thing at night when making a cup of Horlicks, there was the buzz of the old fridge. It was the constant note drawing a circle through his day to which, God willing, he would return. He listened for it now in the early morning; sensed it, felt it, as if to prove to himself that he was still alive. The soft vibration was cold through his bare feet on the kitchen tiles, humming up through his leg bones, his knee replacements, pulsing softly the pistons of his heart, grinding into motion the rusty wheels of his mind.

Turning from the stove he crossed the kitchen, the belt of his blue and purple striped dressing gown tied unevenly, leaving one length dragging on the floor. Slowly, he opened the fridge. The light fell in a long trapezium on the floor. Putting his hand on the small of his back, he groped in the void for eggs and bacon. His daughter, Irene, had gone on at him about it last time she came up from London.

'Dad, let me get you a modern fridge freezer? You won't have to bend so much, or go out into the utility room in the winter for the freezer…'

'It works fine. Don't fuss me!' He remembered wiping the crumbs of the biscuit from the side of his mouth lest they fell onto his cardigan and lay at the mercy of the swiping, patting palm of her hand.

'It'll see me out,' he had said. Young people were always upgrading, wanting something new. He could not tell her that sometimes he thought that the fridge was the life of the house and the day it gave up the ghost, so would he.

He stood at the stove waiting for the oil in the frying pan to heat up. He did not really hear it sizzling, but smelled and saw the acrid haze in the air. Crack, he split the egg, on the side of the work top, a clean, almost break. Raising the egg high, he hung it, letting it drop, ever so slowly, into the pan, then turned and lobbed the shell into the compost bin next to the kitchen sink. Hole in one! Not bad for eighty three. And now for the bacon. He lifted it, sniffing it. Rosamund, his wife, had always been strict about sell-by dates.

It seemed alright and he laid his two rasher ration on either side of the bright eyed yolk. The layout reminded him of a King Charles Spaniel and he half smiled. He had gone back to many of his old army habits since Rosamund died. She had always been bothered about his cholesterol, but in the end she had died first; ironic really, a heart attack, a terrible shock, but merciful and quick.

He heard, or perhaps smelled Foxy coming in from the

garden; the sweet chill of an early morning wrapped in yesterday's warmth. He turned and she seemed to grin, tongue lolling as a fairy tale wolf, trailing the first streaks of sunshine as gold highlights on her mongrel grey coat.

Foxy barked. Was that the phone? It must be. Strange, for no one called these days except the family, and that was always in the evenings. He hacked pre-emptively at the bacon and eggs with a spatula and crossed the kitchen. Picking up the receiver, he put the phone on speaker.

'Good morning Sir Peter!' The voice was faint, crackly like an old radio, but there was no echo.

'Sir Peter?'

'Yes?' He did not recognise the voice and he had not got his hearing aid in.

'Sorry to disturb you so early, Sir. It's the Lodge at College. We've got a letter, from India for you Sir; recorded delivery. Mr Thomas, Taff, Sir, he asked me to call you.'

'Ah yes!'

Taff, the old Welsh guard porter, was about the only one left these days at the College who remembered Sir Peter in his days as Master.

Smoke rose from the bacon and eggs, but the cord on the phone would not allow him to reach to turn them.

'A cordless phone? Shall I get you one for Christmas Dad?' In his head Irene was nagging him again. He stood in the middle of the kitchen angling for the pan with spatula like a child with a fishing net.

'Would you like us to send it on Sir?'

'No, no thank you. I am coming into town this morning. I'll pick it up. Thank you.'

Sir Peter started to cough and flames licked at the left hand ear of the King Charles Spaniel. He shoved the frying pan onto the work top, blowing out the yet timid flame. Damn! The smoke alarm screamed. This he heard, without a doubt and Foxy howled back into the garden, tearing round the stone sundial in manic circles. Sir Peter reached, long armed, over the sink and released the single catch on the kitchen window. Good job he didn't have his hearing aid in. One day he would take the bloody batteries out of both infernal machines. Irene would have an opinion on that too. She had one on everything in her London SW15 way.

At last he switched off the alarm and sat in the silence. The memories came as a wave of dizzy nausea like when he whizzed on a roundabout in Headington Park last summer with Jake, his great grandson; the trees advancing, camouflaged but keeping the line, the ground retreating at speed beneath him.

One, two, three sugars. He clinked the teaspoon on the side of the mug. The tea was evil, sweaty and sweet; of cumin, cinnamon and milk; rancid suet, fire popping eyes, screams and fat dripping human flesh. Unspeakable sights from his last year in India, a beautiful, ancient land that he had loved and that he felt had been betrayed.

This memory, his memory, was delicate and faintly traced in blue and white like grotesque Delft tiles. The Muslim refugees were crowded into coal trucks, cottons puffed with a false breeze flying as flags of surrender over their heads as they cowered under the heat of the day. The journey from Delhi to the Pakistan border that should have taken four hours took four days and he couldn't give them water. There was only enough for his own men and there was a job to do. He was a young Major of the Ninth Gurkha Rifles hanging off the back of the troop carriage as the train pulled into Jullundur station. Just a few sodding miles short of the Pakistan border and they needed to stop for water! He heard them now; hundreds of voices on the platform screeching, shouting, screaming through the clouds of steam. Hindi, Punjabi, Japanese, English, Malay; it made no difference to him. Young as he was he had heard terror in many tongues over the war years and needed no translation. They were baying for blood, this time it was Muslim blood they wanted and they would first rush him and his Gurkhas and then the refugees. Turning back to the troop carriage, he saw Halvidar Rai elbow his way between the men like a powder monkey. Half his size and double his age, sweat was dripping from his hat band into his eyes. He blinked and blinked again, but to no avail and had to lift his hat to wipe his brow with the back of his hand. Now they were both hanging like monkeys off the back of the train and the crowd was pressing closer: steam and smoke, the smell of garlic, urine, tobacco and cordite.

The colour came back to him now; black turbans, trilling pink tongues and the evening sun scything silver crescents from the jumping swords, rifles and blunderbusses.

'Give the order. LLLlet them…' Peter gritted his teeth and slowed his speech to control his stammer, 'ssee the men priming the grenades.' There were ex-military men in the crowd, he thought. Please God let them get the message or there will be a massacre. His men jumped down onto the platform. The double time patter of Gurkha leather boots on the concrete was as welcome to him as early drops of monsoon rain. A roar, as the crowd of faceless faces melted away. The hiss of steam, and the setting sun bleeding life from the day.

That night he had paced the platform, placing a word here or there to the men. God he was tired. This job would be his last job for the Regiment and then his war would be over. The Ninth Gurkha Rifles were going to be part of the Indian Army. He had a place at Oxford to read classics; order and civilization as it ought to be, European style. He couldn't wait. At one end of the platform an old man wasted into the body of a five year old boy rasped and gasped as if the ashes from a fire were being raked out over and over again. There was nothing gentle about his dying. At the other the end, the inconsolable wail of a newborn child, lost as a baby fox in a wood. He lit a cigarette. Tonight thank God, there was no breeze to fan the flames. Cooking fires died in the dust, but bared teeth whispered white among lipless black bearded shadows.

The bacon was what Rosamund used to call crispy, what the children had described as burnt. The egg was shrivelled and charred, the yolk rock hard. He tried HP sauce, squirting it onto the side of the plate, but it didn't make the food look any more appetising. Foxy had returned to try her luck. He let her put her head in his lap, stroking her and feeding her morsels of bacon and egg until they were all gone. She looked at him like a wide eyed toddler, puzzled as when a strict parent suddenly breaks all the rules. The chair scraped on the tiled floor as he got up. Clearing the bile from his throat, his spat into the compost bin.

The grandfather clock at the bottom of the stairs had stopped. He took the little brass key on its knotted string, grey with age, from the nail behind the door, and inserted it into the middle of the clock face. The spring was old and tired of time. It creaked in protest. He pushed the pendulum with his index finger to set it in motion. Tick tock tick tock. The seconds were over-keen running slightly faster than they should, at least for an hour or two. He smiled. At least he has set a purpose to his day. Bing bong bing bong. The clock struck eight. It was too early to go to College yet. If he left it a while there would be an excuse to stay for lunch. The new Master always made him very welcome, and indeed had invited him to move back into College after his wife died.

'You are a valuable member of our community, Sir Peter. You will always have a home here.'

Very kind of course. But old farts should know when to bow out.

In the bedroom he opened the drawer to the bedside table on what used to be Rosamund's side and took out his Gurkha kukri. She had kept it there throughout her illness and he had not moved it since her death. The leather scabbard felt strangely warm. Drawing the curved blade, he looked at himself in it, wishing to see the young officer's grin that Rosamund had fallen in love with. Instead there was an old man who has not yet put his teeth in. He ran the tip of his finger along the blade of the knife. It was still sharp enough to draw blood. He had cut the umbilical cords of both his son and daughter with it, and it had not been used since. Like a blind man, he read his name with his finger, engraved in the handle; Peter 'Robin Hood' Roberts. He smiled. Robin Hood from Roberts, had been his nick name at school. A curse not necessarily a blessing, for idealists don't do very well in the Diplomatic Service. He made a note to get out the polish one winter evening and pushed the blade back into the scabbard.

Back downstairs in the garden Foxy had left two half chewed tennis balls and an orange cricket ball in a line as offerings on the patio. Her master threw the cricket ball over the garden fence to his left. The ball thumped on top of the wheelie bin on the other side and Foxy barked with delight. She was anticipating that the children next door might take her to The Parks to chase their cricket balls.

'Not today old girl!' To make up for it he threw her a soggy tennis ball into the rhododendrons at the back of the garden. But it was not enough, and she whined and begged with big brown eyes when he went out without her to walk to College.

His replacement knees were the first into action with the rest of his joints coming later. Swinging his arms he strode out across The Parks. The breeze rustled the trees which were tipped with copper and gold freshly minted by the sunshine. Sir Peter upped the pace, waiting for the moment his body finally got itself into gear; all the joints and muscles stretched and warm, and for a few minutes at least he moved with the energy of a much younger man.

He was marching now and it felt good. He wondered about the letter and the Regiment and realised it could not be from them. Life moves on. After Indian Independence he had finally gone back to the UK and taken up his place at Oxford, where he had met Rosamund. A quiet Scot, she was reading French and Italian at Somerville. After Oxford he had joined the Diplomatic Service and they had been posted all round the world. He had been tipped for success and had disappointed neither Rosamund nor the Service until the day he had sent an fashionable dispatch from Santiago to London.

'Unwise, ill timed, poor judgement,' people in leather armchairs in London clubs had said.

'Shame! Robbers is a decent chap. One ought to see what can be done.'

And so it came about that in the summer of 1985 Sir Peter, Robin Hood, Roberts had become the new master of his old college in Oxford.

He slowed down, feeling for the bag of bread in his pocket.

There was no Foxy today and the ducks came charging over the grass from the Cherwell.

'Hello chaps! Guess what? It's your ducky day!' He smiled inwardly at his little joke.

The ducks quacked and nipped at his feet, two drakes squabbling over a large morsel.

If the letter were not from the Regiment then who else would write to him from India? The only letters he got these days were bills. There used to be cards at Christmas, but he was pretty much the last one standing of the men from his generation. His inbox too was mostly empty, apart from bridge arrangements and business to do with his position as a Trustee of the Ashmolean Museum.

Idly throwing the bread, he looked towards Rainbow Bridge. The perfect flying arc was broken in two by a falling shadow. The willow on the bank bowed to the water, a heavy steel green. Most people would have seen Monet, but he preferred Turner.

The quacking at his feet stopped. The bread was all gone. He shook out the bag but the ducks were not interested. Disdainful, waggling rears like a gaggle of disappointed shoppers at sale time, they complained their way back to the river.

His stomach rumbled and he remembered that he had given his burnt breakfast to Foxy. Thinking to buy a croissant from the French patisserie on the corner he hurried for the exit from the park.

A chilly gust of wind brought a few leaves down from the trees. They swirled away to lie inside the white posts which roped off the lovingly bedded down cricket pitch. Soon the clocks would go back and the nights would be cold. Suddenly, then, he thought he knew.

The 1985 Year were his boys and girls; his first intake into Woodstock College as Master. They were the Heaven Born, the golden ones and they knew it; a generation in waiting, destined for great things. The children of Thatcher and Reagan, they graduated just as the world was deregulating, opening up. Few had had it so good. But recently their world was turning. Perhaps it was time? Like some mafia Godfather, Oxford always had its way. Sir Peter was no exception. He had come back to Oxford twice; once after the war and again after the Santiago debacle and he would die there. People always returned at some point, even for a day, but in the end they were not visiting Oxford but themselves; two people, the person that they were and the person they had become, face to face across a college dining room table or a quadrangle.

Outside the patisserie, he munched a croissant from a paper bag. The chocolate burst bitter sweet around his mouth just as the pedestrian lights beeped. He crossed with the students, priests and prams, and turning right walked down into town. At the junction there was a girl in a red suede jacket on a bike. Putting her foot down, she waited next to him for the cars heading out of town to pass. Her basket was full of Arabic books, her brown hair tied back in a ponytail, her young face looking forward eagerly, square into the day. He knew her and yet he did not. A blue Volvo passed, except it appeared white. He realised that girl reminded him of Rosamund, as she had used to cycle down from Somerville to Woodstock College to meet him. The girl pushed off. The bike was heavy with the weight of books. Soon she was lost in the morning sun.

Chapter Twelve

Just before he got to the College, Sir Peter wiped the remains of the French breakfast from his mouth with the back of his hand. His mother and daughter would both have chided him. Eating on the street was regarded as common and he chuckled inwardly like a defiant school boy.

He used to think that change was barely perceptible in Oxford, rather like ancient paving stones being worn away by frost, rain and the passage of feet, but not anymore. The need to compete internationally had trumped sentimental reverence for the past. In his days it was just American students that were pandered to. These days all students wanted en-suite bathrooms, college sweat shirts and access to the Internet.

The street in front of his college had been pedestrianised and the new Master must have re-opened the unwinnable war against the dumping of bikes against the wall by the Lodge, for there were no rusty skeletons today. But apart from this, the façade of college was just as it had been on the day of his arrival as an undergraduate in the autumn of 1948 and indeed on the day of his retirement. The small wooden door within the greater one was open and Sir Peter stepped carefully over the high threshold to be greeted by the black and white sign on a T-shaped board.

The College is closed to Visitors

Ignoring it he walked into the Lodge on the right. The old wall and wooden ledged window had been knocked down and replaced by a floor to ceiling glass-fronted room with a desk across the front.

'Like a bloody Novotel!' Sir Peter had once commented in private to another Fellow and member of the ancien régime at a lunch to open the new parts of the building some years ago. He pushed the glass door with the College crest on it and entered the marble floored lodge. The porter, a new man, looked up from his computer screen.

'Can I help you Sir?'

'Is Taff at home?'

Realisation dawned on the porter.

'Ah, Sir Peter, Sir. Nice to meet you. It was me who called you this morning. You look just like your portrait in the dining hall.'

Sir Peter chafed at the Americanism, 'called' not 'phoned,' but nevertheless felt a flutter of excitement at the prospect of banter and the small but enigmatic purpose of his day.

'Mr Jones has the letter Sir. I'll just bleep him.'

Sir Peter turned on his heels looking at the rows of wooden pigeon holes, each one with a student's name on it. Once, just once, he had broken his rule that old farts should know when to bow out, and secretly allied himself with the Junior Common Room in their fight with the new regime to keep the old pigeon holes in the new lodge.

The new marble floor muffled the beat of Taff's familiar marching walk, but the white flame scarred mask, his face, was unchanging.

'From that Indian, Mr Misra, Sir, you remember him?' The two men shook hands and Taff handed him the letter.

'I'll never forget Mr Misra and Miss Angus. Remember the day he turned up here? All puffed up and full of himself, he was!'

'Made quite an entrance I seem to remember. ' Sir Peter laughed for the first time that day, and both men were happier to reminiscence than to talk about themselves.

It was early October 1985 and Sir Peter had been in the Lodge picking up his mail as the students arrived. The girl was there first, shyly picking up her keys and getting directions to her room. Moustache in full bloom, a tall Indian man had banged through the door to the Lodge, grinned, thrown down his suitcase, and looking over the head of the girl announced,

'Misra, Ash Misra. Scholar from India here.'

Sir Peter had raised an eyebrow to Colour Sergeant Taff who, recently invalided out of the Forces after the Falklands War, dealt with the new comer just as he would have an uppity young Rupert fresh out of Sandhurst.

'If you might wait a moment please Sir. Miss Angus was here first.'

Crestfallen, the young Indian was left to jiggle about impatiently from one foot to another and pretend he had not noticed the girl.

Oxford cherishes its ghosts and with an unexpected rush of hope and joy, Sir Peter conjured them in his mind to stand with him now, in the Lodge, just as they had done all those years ago. He thought perhaps that Ash and Isabella had had many names, Tristan and Isolde, Romeo and Juliet, Layla and

Majnun. Age craves the indulgence of perfection and just for a moment they were there; real and unreal, as two young Gods from different stars, their orbits destined to cross but once, perhaps twice, in a millennium. She was a tapestry of red, and gold; a sun bronzed pre-Raphaelite vision of the Virgin Mary, he the blue, black faced lion of a young Krishna painted in gouache. Blinking blue eyes met soft brown ones, within the fraction of knowing without knowing. Perhaps they had been together in some past life; a bejewelled Maharaja with a falcon on his arm and a silver silken Maharani riding out on cocky black and white stallions across the Punjab hills? It was as it had been and always would be.

She looked down. He looked away.

The girl had finished signing in with Taff and stood to one side putting her paper work in order. Methodically, Taff ticked his file and turned his attention to the boy from Delhi University.

A promising scholar and a fine cricketer and gentleman. The list of the young man's sporting and other achievements in the scholarship application that Sir Peter had rubber stamped himself ran over several pages; winner, captain first XI, senior house captain, all India under eighteens, and so on and so forth, collapsing into a cascade of impressive roman numerals and dates which he and probably no one else ever bothered to read.

'We take one from Delhi every year,' the out-going Master had said to Sir Peter at their handover lunch. 'Good lads. Fine sportsmen. Never any problems.'

The girl crossed the room to check her pigeon hole. It was stuffed with welcome material from the Junior Common Room. She has medieval hands, Sir Peter had thought, thin, already returned to winter white, while the rest of her was soft brown from the summer sun. He wanted to reach out and touch her fine golden hair which hung loose down the back of her black polo neck jumper, almost wet with sheen. Her face was still that of a child, full and round. She reminded him of his own daughter at that age. He wondered if she knew how perfect she was, too perfect perhaps to be beautiful. He nodded, smiled and met her eye and knew that she did not.

By then Mr Misra had his room keys and dithered from left to right foot and back again and grinned before striding out of the lodge. The three of them, Taff, Isabella and Sir Peter stared at his blue and brown checked suitcase abandoned by the door. It had two green Air India tags tied to the handle with string and a shiny new purple leather name tag holder with his name printed neatly in it in black capitals.

Taff rolled his eyes to the ceiling.

'And just who the devil does he think is going to take that up to his room ? Porters we are, not servants!'

'He'll come back for it soon enough.' Sir Peter had quipped and the girl had giggled shyly and smiled.

Chapter Thirteen

'Are you staying for lunch Sir? ' Taff enquired of his former boss.

'Might as well see what the revolutionaries have been up too now I am here!'

'Good! Then you'll have time for a coffee?'

Sir Peter laughed again.

'Still making that potion then Taff?'

The two men pushed through the door at the back of the lodge to the porter's office.

'Glad to see they left you some privacy.' Despite the glass and marble façade the porters' back office had not changed much. The second hand of the big white clock on the wall still limped and shuddered to mark time, but had been joined by a flat screen computer and a microwave oven. The mid-morning sun streamed in shafts through the grilled arched window high up to the street and tiny particles of gilded dust rode the warm thermals. The telephone directories, box files, biscuit tins, tea and coffee still stood, ordered, on shelves next to the key cupboard, and the *Daily Mail* was read but neatly folded on the corner of Taff's desk.

'Still got my coffee pot too. Always do our best for tradition in the Porters' Mess.' Taff proffered a battered old jug towards Sir Peter.

'And never washed yet, I hope?' Sir Peter stuck his nose towards the pot to check that it was still encrusted with black coffee inside. 'Good, then I should very much like a cup. Still got your old chair too.' Stiffly he lowered himself into a grubby looking armchair set to catch the falling halo of sunshine from the window.

'Caused no end of trouble that chair did; breaks all the rules in the book it does. Not up to fire regulation standards. One day they wanted to take it away. Last straw it was for me. I came on all Colour Sergeant Taff and said if you throw out the bloody chair I go with it. So they let me keep it. I retire next week you know. That makes twenty-five years keeping this place running!'

'College won't be the same without you. You've always run a tight ship.' Taff sucked his teeth by way of a grin and busied himself with his famous coffee ritual. As the son of an Italian ice-cream maker born and brought up in the Rhondda Valley, coffee making was indeed a serious addiction he had inherited, most likely intravenously, while still in the womb.

'Fancy that boyo Misra getting in touch. Wonder what they are up to now, Mr Misra and Miss Angus? A and M we nick-named them in the Lodge back in the day. Students were always in here, collecting their post after breakfast, after lunch, after dinner. Regular rugby scrum it was round the pigeon holes in those days. It's all gone now of course; more is the loss. Pigeon hole love affairs! Social media has done for that. The new Master says that whole University would grind to a halt without it. Sad it is. A and M, we porters watched their whole romance play out in front of our eyes that year. He'd sneak in bright and early all sheepish, and put a note for her in her pigeonhole. Later she would arrive and raise her eyes to the heaven, tut tut, and blush. Then blow me down one day she came and put a note in for him! I remember it particular like because we had bets on it and I won a tenner. Should have seen Mr Misra's face that day, Sir! Wobbled his head in that funny way he had when playing the fool and winked at me! Then there was that dreadful day, and then the long summer with him in his cricket whites and them two glued to each other at the hip laughing and waving, 'Hello Colour Sergeant Taff,' every time they passed the Lodge.

Taff heated some milk in the microwave, poured the steaming coffee into two mugs, handed one to Sir Peter and parked himself on the corner of his desk. His old photo was still there too; a bedraggled Young Taff standing with a group of grinning Welsh guards, bare torso-ed after crossing the Equator on the flight deck of the Sir Galahad on the way to the Falklands. The picture had faded a little over the years. Taff was one of the lucky ones who had survived the bombing in Stanley Harbour with severe burns and shrapnel wounds in his left leg.

Cautiously Sir Peter sipped the coffee, anticipating the tingling of caffeine in his head and toes.

'Taff, you and I have seen many students pair off over the years but I always felt there was something special about those two. They were different, so intense somehow, though I could never put a finger on anything.'

Sir Peter cradled the warm coffee mug to his lips. He was remembering far too much that morning, and now, for the second time, it was his Santiago dispatch.

The papers were still under the 30 year rule and bound by the Official Secrets Act, but time had eventually passed a favourable verdict on him, and in fairness the Former Secretary of State had had the good grace to invite him to lunch.

Taff changed the subject. 'Funny to think of that lot running the country! Every time I put on the telly one or other of them pops up. That Joanna what's her name was all glammed up on 'Question Time' the other night. Always running for some post or other she was. I remember one day her pigeon hole was bursting at the seams with letters and campaign flyers.

'I bet the Prime Minister gets less post than you!' I said and she shrugged her shoulders and flicked her hair.

'One day Taff, I'll find out!'

'And then there was that chap from British Fuels; vomited in the fountain after a boat club dinner. Told him to clean it out. And that Chinaman too I remember. Dark horse that one. Never said much. We called him Bruce Lee.'

Sir Peter smiled but was still brooding.

'Penny for your thoughts. Sir?' Taff grimaced a terrifying grin. Then suddenly, out of the blue, 'It comes to us all you know.'

'What does?'

'Failure.' The old Welshman took a deep breath. 'I never went back into the Sir Galahad. I had friends still trapped down in that accursed ship but I couldn't face the flames. But there were lads who did and when I came home I was fêted as a hero.'

For a long while Sir Peter said nothing, giving the old soldier's confession the reverence it required.

'Perhaps none of us ever measures up to the man we had hoped to be.'

A taxi honked outside the window, the driver obviously impatient. Taff looked at the clock and then at the letter from India. It was bulky as if it contained something of importance and it rested unopened on the arm of Sir Peter's chair. Sir Peter knew the nosey old Welshman was dying to know what was inside!

The letter was addressed, as if in haste, in a scrawling black ballpoint pen. The stamps were stuck on higgledy piggledy, two underneath three, and postmarked New Dehli, 29th September 2010. Later that evening Sir Peter would remove the stamps to add to the collection he had been keeping since he was a boy. He looked at the back of the letter. Ash Misra had just written his name. Apparently return addresses were going out of fashion, rather like honour, morality and wisdom.

Suddenly, Sir Peter felt weary. The pain in his hip made him wince as he tried to get out of the chair. After lunch he would read newspapers in the Senior Common Room and get a taxi home. He would open the letter in private that evening.

Chapter Fourteen

Sir Peter arrived at College on Sunday morning just as the mist was lifting, to peals of the chapel bells. He doubted very much that Isabella would show up and had brought Foxy with him for the walk so that he had an excuse for not going to church. He meandered in and out of the maze garden then back into the front quad. There were still a few roses and a hint of fragrance in the air. He wondered what he on earth he was doing there. He knew he was lonely in old age with nothing better to do. But it was more than that. He felt responsible even after all these years, responsible for Ash and Isabella, what had happened that winter night, and perhaps even a little for India, for the horrific events all those years ago when he was a young Gurkha officer. God knew he and his men had done their best, but their best had not been good enough. No one's had.

The last of the worshippers went in for Communion and the College clock struck a smart eleven. He heard her before he saw her, the soft tip tap of heels on the flagstones in the Lodge. She stopped briefly looking around her for Ash. Then she wandered timidly out in the quad as if cast adrift, a tiny, slim figure in a neatly belted camel coloured coat and knee length brown suede boots.

'Miss Angus, good morning,' Sir Peter called softy, stepping forward and removing his hat so that she might more easily recognise him. She jumped, eyes wide, startled and he saw that her face was pinched with cold and there were bags under her eyes as if she had not slept well. She squinted up at him against the autumn sun, her red hair cropped shorter now, curling with the morning damp. She had aged of course but for him, she was still impossibly young.

'Sir Peter, I was just… What a surprise! No one's called me Miss Angus in years!' Her face was tight with anxiety, fear even and he reached forward gently touching her hand in its orange leather glove.

'I brought this,' he said quickly, 'a letter from Mr Misra in New Delhi.' She turned pale, the blood draining from her face

Sir Peter took her to The Tack Room for coffee. The staff turned a blind eye to Foxy's presence, even sneaking him a bowl of water, provided Sir Peter kept him discreetly next to their corner table. He was doubly glad that he had brought the dog, for Foxy seemed to help Isabella relax and facilitated conversation. Inside in the warm room, Isabella's cheeks flushed pink again. Ash's letter had contained a note to Sir Peter and another sealed letter to Isabella. In the note Ash had explained in a very matter of fact way, as it were the most normal thing in the world, that twenty-five years ago he and Isabella had arranged to meet this weekend in Oxford. Unfortunately, his mother had died recently and he was currently in New Delhi for her funeral and to attend to her affairs. Ash doubted that Isabella would remember their planned meeting and had tried in vain to find her on the Internet. He was therefore taking the liberty of sending a letter to her care of Sir Peter at the College trusting to fate that somehow she might receive it. All this Sir

Peter had told Isabella at College, wanting to ease her evident anxiety. Now she sipped her coffee, stroked Foxy's velvety head and asked him about his family then told him about her sons and her art. Watching her, Sir Peter was suddenly inexplicably angry with Ash for letting her down.

Afterwards Isabella put her un-opened letter into her handbag and walked with Sir Peter and Foxy back to The Parks. He felt sad when it was time to part for he had enjoyed the young woman's company.

'Be careful, is it wise?' He had wanted to warn her, but was it any of his business? So he said nothing.

Chapter Fifteen

New Delhi, Mid October 2010

Ash was petrified. He stared at the scorpion, the shadow of it, stark black, its claws huge, wide open. It was famished, desperate, ready to pounce.

He ought to sleep well in Delhi, after all it was supposed to be home, yet he never did. There was always the distant battle of car horns in the early morning, and the sunshine crept around the edges of the blinds. Ash awoke with a start to the smell of alcohol and heavy perfume. The woman slept on her front, snuggled up to him, the tattoo of the scorpion on her upper right arm just below his pillow. Oh hell! he thought, then, did we? His mind jerked into gear. She had arrived late the previous night, after a charity event, a little drunk. There had been the usual emotion and tears; her son in New York and his bitch of a girlfriend, her husband, the media, everyone conspiring against her. She had been in a state. No, he remembered. They hadn't, thank God, but when he had suggested that she perhaps she ought to think about seeing a doctor she had gone into melt down. Ash was her only friend in the world. What would she do without him? He had wiped her face with a warm damp flannel as if she had been a little girl, and put her to bed with her underclothes clothes on. They had indeed slept together in the emperor sized bed, chastely as brother and sister. He looked at her now, Roopa, known as Roo, lying there all skin and bones. The poor scorpion which had once been the trade mark of a moderately successful and extremely voluptuous actress turned PR guru, hung slack and sagging on her half-starved arm. Ash and Roopa had played together as children. He had been the Tigger to her Roo. Hide and seek and climbing trees had been their favourite games but she had always been the braver and more nimble one, teasing him from the high branches. Their mothers had been school friends and the two families were said to be related in some way, although neither Ash nor Roo had ever been sure exactly how. They had fallen into bed together after a family wedding in Dubai some ten years ago. Ash had got into the habit of calling her up every time he was in Delhi and she would reciprocate when she was in Dubai, which conveniently for him was seldom. She was married of course and their affair had gone on in hotel bedrooms for about seven years. Her weight had seesawed over the years too, up after the children were born, down and up again when her husband was implicated in a corruption scandal. It had entered the anorexic phase few years previously when she started her own media and PR agency and that was when the drinking had taken hold. They had ceased to be lovers three years ago and had only met in public at the funeral ceremonies on this trip. But her texts had become more frequent, emotional and demanding. Ash was afraid she wanted to start things up again. He had always felt uncomfortable about the whole thing, uneasy, guilty, about playing too close to home. Foreign girls were fair game. Indian ones, especially 'sisters' were not.

Quietly, he slipped out of the bed and went across to the bathroom. Closing the door, he put on the light and turned on the basin tap, splashing his face with cold water. Ash, you bloody fool! Raising his head, he confronted himself in the bathroom mirror. It hit him like a slap in the face. His face was rough with stubble. He was no longer handsome and dashing, no longer young. A tired middle aged man who resembled his father stared back at him. His hair was more grey than black, his cheeks puffy and the skin under his eyes was starting to turn purple. The thick ebony eyebrows that had once so enchanted the girls were now too thick and wiry, forbidding, slightly sinister, untrustworthy, stern.

Sighing, he began to shave and when he was done, he tiptoed back into the bedroom just as his Blackberry bleeped on the bedside table. Damn! He wanted to make a quick get-away. Roo stirred in her sleep, snoring gently as she rolled over to what had been his side of the bed.

'Ash?

'I'm here baby.' He called them all baby. It reduced the margin for error.

'Come back to bed!' she coaxed.

'I can't,' he replied finally emerging from the bathroom and putting on his trousers. 'I'm meeting Vikram at the Golf Club. Gotta roll!'

She sat up, pulling the sheet around her as if she were cold and he hastily collected up his personal things. His mother's funeral rites had all been completed and her apartment finally sold. Everything that needed to be done had been done, and he was booked on the afternoon flight back to Dubai. Seeing Roo sitting there half-naked in the cruel light of day, he was shocked. She had had a face lift a few years ago and now with age, alcohol and excessive dieting she resembled an emaciated guinea pig. She looked so ill, he did not want to hurt her or trigger a further bout of last night's histrionics, so he negotiated a gentle retreat, urging her once more at the last to please see a doctor.

Downstairs in front of the hotel he helped the chauffeur pack his suitcase and golf clubs into the trunk of the Mercedes. The clubs were the only thing he had taken from his mother's place. The proceeds of his share of the estate had gone to his sister's children. He had made more than enough money and wanted none of it. His generosity with his share of the inheritance had placated his sister who had called him in Dubai three weeks ago and told him in no uncertain terms that their mother was dying, really dying at last. Ash had always been Mataji's favourite, spoilt and indulged, and she, his sister, was fed up to the back teeth of bearing the burden alone. He had always put himself first. She had made it clear that it was time to bloody well grow up, stop shirking his duty, get back to Delhi and spend some time with Mataji before it was too late.

In the back of the Mercedes Ash busied himself with his emails on his Blackberry, except that there weren't many these days and he soon gave up the pretence, gazing out of the window instead. It was early but the infamous Delhi traffic roared and honked, peeped and beeped its way through the mist and smog. The imperturbable driver took the chaos in his stride, his eyes flitting from a scooter in his rear view mirror to three filthy children the eldest of whom could not have been more than four years old, launching themselves off the central reservation at the traffic lights to beg. It wasn't long before they pecked and tweeted at Ash's window like little birds, grubby ones, in plastic flip flops. He opened it half way and reaching out his hand, gave them each a hundred rupees.

'Thank you Sir, Come back another day, not forgetting me.' The smallest boy lisped, head on one side, cute as his minders had no doubt taught him to be. But his eyes behind were dead. Ash looked sharply away, scratching his neck, swallowing hard to swallow the stench, the unforgettable stench that would never leave him, garlic burning flames choking in his chest as he ran. He itched again, ragged at the edges after all that had happened in the last few weeks. He hated Delhi, despised the place. It oozed and seethed and whenever he returned, he was tense, on edge and short tempered. He could never get away quickly enough and yet the place was part of him. Perhaps he loved the city after all? Despite himself, despite everything, Delhi had always conspired to draw him back and always there was that hunger, a thirst, for that familiar smell of family cooking that was never the same in anyone else's house, that gentle loving voice, that feeling of comfort and belonging that people call home.

He had lived in many places over the years, Oxford, London, New York, Mumbai and Dubai. But this city was really many different cities all in one. At every corner he would bump-up against his former self, a young man full of hope and dreams, smart, dapper with his ridiculous moustache who thought he was special, marked out for great things. Now he was the ghost of himself browsing the bookshops in Khan Market, and there he was again, the smell of hot oil sizzling in the pan, eating sticky sweet jaleebis with a big breasted, pigtailed girl from the south he had once known. Driving along that morning he recognised many versions of himself and at the same time did not. This was hardly surprising for he barely knew himself some days. He was always moving, never still, as if the faster he ran the safer he would be. In Delhi he was frustrated by the old ways that barely changed, smoothed over here and there with a veneer of marble and glass and what seemed to him a pretence of modernity and progress. He was seduced by the familiar, yet repulsed and disgusted by it at the same time. It was a circle he had tried to square many times in his own head without success. In consequence, he came back to Delhi as infrequently as possible over the years; duty visits to his mother, family weddings he could not avoid, a funeral or two, work trips, always pleading the imperative of a pressing new business deal to minimise the time spent at the old family home. He would focus on the job in hand, get it done and jump on the first plane back to Dubai as quickly as possible. That way he avoided the fire, minimised the pain.

Chapter Sixteen

'Man, you played shite today.' Vikram leaned back in his chair and roared with laughter.

'Don't complain, you won!' Ash responded in kind.

There was a pause. Vikram was no fool. 'These things, take time you know. When my Mom passed away it was…'

Ash cut him short. They were cousins, and knew far too much about skeletons in family cupboards for comfort.

'Mataji had the funeral she wanted. Everyone was there…' Ash circled his right hand up to the ceiling. And that was it on the subject, nothing more to be said.

The two cousins were sitting at the window of the bar in the Delhi Golf Club eating brunch. There was a reassuring smell of beer, cooking oil and furniture polish that disguised the lurking threat of damp and mould. To Ash's Dubai accustomed eye, the red leather chairs and mahogany tables were tatty and old, like the two retired Indian Air Force officers who sat nearby in their turbans. They seemed to have taken root as gnarled tree trunks in their potted tub chairs. Ash sipped his tea staring at the peacock strutting across the 18th fairway as if he were the Emperor of India.

'Time to get married Bro.' Vikram chuckled, his mouth full of egg and mushrooms. 'Give it another go! Look at me.' He patted his belly with satisfaction. 'Hasn't done me any harm!'

Ash looked as he was bidden surveying the balding, grey haired middle aged man bulging out of his magenta coloured golf shirt and laughed. Vikram had turned out to be the antithesis of Ash who had become the black sheep of the family. His cousin had done everything by the book, the exams, the arranged marriage, and a plum career in the Indian Administrative Service and it had all worked out. Ash thought of Priyanka, Vikram's plain, kind wife who was rolling into middle age in her gloriously expanding saris. She barely changed, family was her world and she saw no need to look beyond it for fulfilment. And there were their two chubby kids, the girl still at school, the boy at university in the USA. To Ash, Vikram was everything he hadn't wanted to be, and terrifyingly the symbol of what he might have become if he had stayed in India. He thought of the India he had left behind with its musty single fanned offices and fax machines, the endless circumlocution and bureaucracy. In the early days in Dubai there simply hadn't been any rules. Sure, it was all about who you knew but it had been fast, furious and deadly with one end in sight; money and lots of it. It had been like the Wild West, every man for himself. He had been free of family and obligations, free to see who he liked, sleep with whom he liked, free to live on his wits, ride the wave and whether he won or lost, it had been up to him.

'Don't you get lonely, Bro living alone?' Vikram persisted in a sympathetic mode. 'I mean, I know you get to bed all those exotic bikini babes; white, black, yellow, brown. I bet you've had them all.'

But Ash was not in the mood.

'I'm fine,' he said. All this banter was code for the financial crisis. He knew his cousin was trying to be kind but there was a rivalry between them. There always had been. Vikram was jealous of the money Ash had made in Dubai and there was a hint of glee and triumph when he talked about the recent crash. Perhaps it vindicated his own choice of bureaucracy over business.

'Don't worry about me, man. I'm alright.' That was not really what Vikram wanted to hear and Ash knew it.

'Why don't you come home, back to India? I could speak to a few guys I know.

But Ash felt a rising sense of panic, a choking suffocation at the thought of it and was ashamed of himself. Didn't Vikram realise that Ash considered himself international now, rather than simply Indian. Twenty years in Dubai had changed him and frankly, deep down inside, he felt he was too good for India. There was no way he would come back. He just couldn't contemplate it, and the mere idea of it made him clench his fists, tight with anger and despair.

Ash was boarding his flight when his Blackberry beeped. Old habits die hard. Slickly, he unholstered the phone from his belt, cocking it to his ear with a rush of adrenalin as if hustling a deal.

'Hello, Ash?' There was a pause, a long, long pause that seemed to stretch back eons of time but he knew who it was before she spoke.

'It's Isabella.' It was as if he had been most lovingly and tenderly kicked in the stomach. His breath caught in his chest and he was overwhelmed with a scent of lemons.

'Hello,' he teased, mimicking her British accent and was

relieved to hear her laugh. Her response tickled down the line and immediately it was as if they were back in College snuggled under the old blue blanket. 'Yes, it's me. His voice squeaked upwards with sudden emotion.

'I got your letter.' She said, slowly, anxiously.

'Really? That's amazing. I just…'

'Sir Peter gave it to me. He…'She too was lost for words and it occurred to Ash that perhaps Isabella had remembered. Had she actually turned up? The idea of her waiting for him alone in the Lodge left him dazed.

'I'm so sorry. I couldn't make it. My mother has just died. We were in the middle of the funeral and all.' Ash explained as he had done in his letter to her.

'It's OK. I understand. I'm sorry for your loss.'

'Thank you, Isabella. She had not been herself for some time. Dementia is a cruel disease.' Ash wondered why he had written to Isabella about that. His mother's Alzheimer's had been a closely guarded family secret.

There was another pause, and they embraced the silence, the wonder of it, the miracle of reaching out, touching, after so long.

'Anyways, how are you?' Ash managed at last.

'Well, well. I'm married with teenage twins. Two boys. I'm an artist.'

The tannoy blared with the last call for the flight. The stewardess stared at him primly like a school mistress.

'Can you turn your phone off please, Sir?'

'Listen Isa, I'm just boarding a flight to Dubai. I'm an investment banker. Divorced, a long ways back, no kids. It's great to be connected. Can I revert to you tonight?

And that was it. The line dropped and his heart sank. Ash was exhausted, overgrown with the business of life, yet the mere sound of her voice from thousands of miles away beamed off a satellite in space, had cut back the undergrowth and opened up some primeval pathway etched on the core of his soul.

CHAPTER SEVENTEEN

Dubai, Mid October 2010

In the luggage hall, Ash was walking through a lemon grove, all the people were trees, their chatter a breeze rustling the leaves; Assssh, Assssh, they seemed to call. He was looking for a girl with a porcelain face and a twist of golden hair and he was young again, his heart playing Bach, bizarrely beating the din ta din of a tabla beat.

His Blackberry buzzed, interrupting his reverie. For once he ignored it but it buzzed again with another message. She had sent several while he was in the air.

'Coucou mon doudou, I'm here! : -)

Solonge, damn! He had been seeing her for five months now and she had started calling him Doudou about eight weeks ago. The pet name snagged and snared like a tiny fish hook in his skin. He had forgotten that she would be at the airport or rather neglected her messages in the hope that she might not show up.

But there she was, tall and elegant behind the barrier in the arrivals hall, her long black curls brushing her shoulders, beautifully made up for the evening but covered for modesty's sake in a long black abbaya. Impossibly high heeled velvet shoes with sparkling crystal clasps peeked out at the hem. Damn it! Solonge had made an effort for him and she would be wearing something exciting underneath, a chic and seductive number no doubt.

'Hello Doudou,' she greeted him with a perfect French smile, careful not to touch him in public but with her head artfully dipped to the right by way of invitation. 'Did you forget? It's Bettina's leaving party tonight. I sent you a million messages on Facebook but you never replied.' She pouted.

'Solange, you know I'm not interested in all that Facebook stuff.'

She sniffed, jerking up her head, injured by his sharp response, then, thinking better of it, reached out to try and brush his hand. She failed.

'Forgive me Doudou. How stupid and selfish I am! I was just trying to help, to support.' Ash knew that all too well. Women always wanted to do that to him, take him under their wing, and Solonge was a nice woman, kind and concerned about him and his mother. She always meant well, but it had got to the stage in the relationship when an emotional investment would be required on his part rather than socialising and sex. It wouldn't be long before the 'M' and 'B' words began to crop up. That was precisely why he had not replied to her messages.

But Ash was not made of stone and seeing that she was hurt, he relented.

'No. It's my fault. I'm just not in the mood for a party.' They were walking toward the taxis now and she came close so that the back of her hand made contact with his.

'No of course you're not. So insensitive of me! We don't have to go. Though I will have to pop in myself at some point.' She pronounced insensitive in the French way which he had once found so alluring. 'It's just I thought it might cheer you up now you are out of mourning. You were always such an extrovert. Doudou my party boy!'

Another hook tore a little nick in his flesh but he felt guilty for ignoring Solonge while he was in Delhi.

'Have you eaten, Babe?' He said trying to smile.

'Non.' She replied deliberately petulant like a child.

'How about I call *Tao* and see if we can get us that window table.' It was a super expensive place and where they had gone on their first date. They would have a pleasant meal and he would end it afterwards, on good terms, friends on an all options basis in the usual Dubai expat way.

The restaurant was dark, renowned for its hushed air of discretion that reflected power, money and sex. But tonight it was at risk of slipping into melancholic gloom. Something had changed in Ash too. He was weary, weary of the game, the constant chasing, the fear of missing the boat, of getting left behind. Hurry! Close that deal! On to the next and then the next, always wanting more and for what? That night he just wanted to slink away into the shadows, to hide, to be unseen. On the 27th floor of a prestigious five star hotel, the elite eating establishment was fitted out with shiny mahogany panels cut out with the ubiquitous round Chinese symbol. Ash presumed it had something to do with prosperity and good fortune. The restaurant was half empty, the other diners mostly middle aged men like Ash of various nationalities with glamorous young women at their sides. The men's pudgy hands and wrists were adorned with chunky gold rings and designer watches. Their companions were, without exception, tall, thin, elegant and sleek with gym-toned arms and thighs, like thoroughbred race-horses. How ridiculous the men all looked with young women in tow, many of whom could have been their daughters. Ash shuddered at the realisation that this category now included him; a washed up, burnt out middle aged man who partied with ambitious, nubile women nearly half his age. The restaurant boasted delicacies from the East; fine Asian cuisine, a top chef poached from the Mandarin Oriental in Hong Kong, and diminutive Filipina waitresses in tight red silk cheongsams temptingly slit high on the thigh. At the height of the financial boom it has been almost impossible to get a table at *Tao*. That night Ash had obtained an excellent table overlooking the Gulf with ease.

Solonge had removed her abbaya. She was perfect; the clinical alignment of her super white teeth, the slick poppy red lipstick, dramatic but not too bright, the slope of her shoulders and curve of her olive skinned breasts in her velvet midnight blue cocktail dress, her tiny diamond earrings, and solitary gold bangle around her wrist. She might have stepped out of the pages of a glossy European life style magazine. And yet with her carefully highlighted eye-brows and dramatic eye make-up, she was so flawless that she might have been any woman at all. Ash observed her as she studied the wine menu with an air of superiority and erudition. Born in Paris and educated at the Sorbonne, she worked in the cultural section of the French Embassy and was engaged on some secret museum project in the Emirates. She was simply stunning, a seductive cocktail of charm, education and intelligence. Everything about her oozed taste, a rare quality in Dubai. And she was young too, although not that young. At thirty two and divorced, her time was running out. Career wasn't enough and she was hunting for a mate. Ash was damned if he were going to fall into that trap.

You only had to stroll around the Marina on a winter Saturday morning to view the ridiculous bands of harassed looking fifty year old businessmen and bankers. With gritted teeth they dragged or chased precocious toddlers on or in an assortment of push bikes, scooters and red, yellow and purple plastic cars.

Ash thought that all the educated expats in Dubai were running away from something; a divorce, a bankruptcy, a prosecution, a war, a corrupt and efficient state, fear, grief, guilt, running from themselves, their failures, their secrets or just their own mediocrity. They were all carpetbaggers, opportunists, every one of them, including himself.

Solonge chose the lobster noodles washed down with a Chablis, as he knew she would, and he opted for teriyaki beef. Heresy it might be, but after nearly a month on a vegetarian diet in India, he craved it; thin and tender, cooked in in a fizzing second on the hot plate in the Japanese way. He salivated at the thought of the juices running in his mouth.

'C'est terrible.' Solange was swilling her wine in the glass savouring the bouquet with the air of a connoisseur. 'Everywhere people are packing up and leaving. The other night at dinner, eight out of the ten around the table had been made redundant.' She clicked her fingers. 'Just like that, overnight. Ce n'est pas juste.' She shrugged her shoulders and raised her hands in a very Gallic gesture of despair.

A violin sounded softly in Ash's head along with the fetid stink of damp trainers and sweaty rowing kit left to dry on the radiators in College. He tried to concentrate, to pull himself back.

'What goes up must come down.' He replied without enthusiasm. 'We were all conned by our own illusions. Not as invincible as we thought.' In truth he had not seen it coming, the financial crash. Even when Lehman Brothers had collapsed he had not drawn the dots to see how it would impact on business in the Middle East. And then one Saudi investor in particular had disappeared overnight. No one knew where the money had gone and that had been the beginning of the end in his own line of work.

They stared out at the Arabian night, the lights like multiple strings of diamonds adorning the coast, here and there a twinkling ruby or emerald, a buoy, ships at sea. His head pealed with chapel bells. Oxford early on a Sunday morning just as the mist was lifting…

Solonge tried hard that evening, Ash had to admit. She recounted with enthusiasm and much pouting and flicking of hair tales of her childhood in France and the large family holiday house near Nice. Valiantly, she tried to draw Ash out of himself even suggesting that she might forego Bettina's party and inviting him back to her place. But Ash's mind was elsewhere, dizzy with citrus scent, all the time Isabella's voice, whispering in his ear.

'Ash, Ash, can you hear me?'

Conversation with Solange meandered around but, unfed by him, it petered out, leaving them with the tinkling sound of a water feature in the centre of the restaurant. It was a relief to them both when Ash dropped Solonge off at her friend's place, kissing her once on each cheek.

'Take care, Ash Misra.' She patted his shoulder affectionately but with an air of finality. 'Call me, you know where I am.' He did not promise that he would.

CHAPTER EIGHTEEN

Ash's penthouse apartment was stifling yet a strange breeze blew in the stillness. He felt an imaginary wisp of Isabella's golden hair soft against his face, so real that he brushed it away with the back of his hand. As instructed, his daily house boy had left the air conditioning on low while his master had been away, but it was as if all the heat of the last weeks was stored in the airless rooms. Ash's head thumped, wild with memories; the sweet scent of tea on Isa's breath, the tips of her fingers moving tenderly over his face, the soft rasping, cut, cut of the razor, the crack of the willow on leather. His mother singing *Vaishava Jana Tod*, quietly, in the early morning when she thought no one was listening. A vision of two butterflies; English red admirals, black, red, yellow and gold, fluttering, dancing, settling on the purple buddleia in the College garden. Ash turned his attention to the air conditioning. He wanted to be cold, really cold, the kind of cold that claws cheeks and bites to the bone, vicious bitter cold that knocks the breath out of you so you cannot think. He turned the air con to full blast, clicking the icon to the snowflake, and went to pour himself a whisky

Although Ash possessed a domestic liquor licence it was mainly for the purposes of entertainment. People might have accused him of various vices over the years but drink was not one of them. He did however enjoy a single malt from time to time and blamed Sir Peter Roberts for the habit. The old Master had introduced Ash to the joys of a wee fireside dram when he and his wife had invited him to their home for Christmas all those years ago.

It was nearly midnight. Ash stood alone at the panoramic floor to ceiling windows, swirling his whisky in a crystal glass. In front of him, above and below, the enchanted palaces of Dubai flaunted themselves in all their electric glory, amongst them the shadowy skeletons of unfinished buildings abandoned overnight when the cash had run dry, the mighty cranes hanging over them like hangmen's gibbets. He reached out his hand to touch the window, pushing in pretence at the building opposite as if it might be a domino he could topple to start a cascade. And yet this city of light, sun, glitzy, glass and chrome was a wizard with mystical powers. Was there no end to its miracles; water into wine, sand into gold, beggars into kings? And it was his city. He had built half the damn place! Ash could point out all the buildings to you. He had seen most of them going up. He could reel off the names of all the mega projects he had been involved in financing, the ones that had come to fruition, the ones that had not, the ones that were jerry built and the ones that were not; malls, golf courses, movie studios, ice rinks, ice palaces, ski domes, Venetian villas, towers, skyscrapers, underwater hotels. Twenty plus years of brokering, haggling, bestowing the billions as if they were fairy dust conjured out of thin air.

Ash sipped his whisky waiting for its numbing hit and began to laugh, a big belly aching chuckle. It was all so utterly absurd and the funniest thing of all was that they had actually begun to believe in their own follies, that they might actually be worth the gargantuan salaries they were being paid and that the insane feeding frenzy would continue without end. No one had known where fantasy stopped and reality started. No one had asked where all the capital was coming from and how it would ever be paid back. But now the music had stopped, the game was over and they had all been caught with their pants down.

Ash had no sympathy for himself and wanted none from others. He had done a deal with the devil and he knew it. Yes, he had stored up a crock of gold for himself, every cent of it tax free. But Dubai afforded him no formal rights, no vote, no citizenship, nor meaningful right of abode to call home. At the end of the day he was a migrant worker just like all the rest. But hell! Who needed rights? He laughed again, wicked and hollow sounding in the marble floored apartment. Two years tax free in this place and he had already made enough to buy citizenship anywhere he liked, anywhere in the world.

The whisky in his glass burnt orange in the city lights, Glenlivet, his favourite. For some reason the smell reminded him of wood smoke and damp leaves fallen on rain washed pavements. Again an imaginary curl of Isabella's hair tickled his cheek. This time he did not brush it away. He had never forgotten, always wondered about her. In the early years after Oxford, he would wake to the creak of a floorboard and see her standing there at the door to his College room with snowflakes in her hair. And there had been times when he had felt her close, looking for her face in the Dubai moon, wondering if she could hear him or see him back. He would hear her in the lilt of a newsreader's voice or a snippet of forgotten melody, glimpse her in the turn of a stranger's head or a fleeting smile, a scent of lemons like the perfume she used to wear, an invisible shadow always, never there. What had she been doing all these years while he was building castles in the desert sand?

Ash started to shiver, his teeth chattering with cold. Never look back! That was his mantra. That was how he survived. Going to the bedroom he wrapped himself in a quilt, hesitated, then picked up the phone.

CHAPTER 19

Yorkshire Dales, late autumn 2010

Ash was lost. The GPS had dropped just after he had turned off the motorway. Isabella had warned him that this might happen, but he had not brought a map. He parked the rented silver Mercedes on the cobbles in the shadow of the ruined castle, which presented itself like a picture postcard in the autumn sunshine. Having left London late morning, surely he wasn't far from Isa's farmhouse now? All was quiet and still in the little Yorkshire market town, and as he got out of the car, the beep of his electronic key seemed to offend the day.

Ash strode into the little newsagent's to ask the way, the bell tinkling at the door as he entered, making him think of his mother, the stores in Delhi when he was child and how warm and safe his tiny hand had always felt in hers. To his surprise there were three other people in the newsagent's and he had to wait his turn. They paid no heed to him, as if a tall Indian dressed in Levi jeans with a yellow spotted handkerchief carefully folded in the breast pocket of his tweed jacket, were quite a normal part of the Yorkshire scene.

The girl behind the counter was a terrifying sight, with bright purple hair, black lipstick and an assortment of studs all the way up her left ear. A Goth, he remembered was the name for such fashion. What on earth possessed young English people to dress from head to toe in black like that: he had never understood it. But no one seemed give her a second glance.

'Excuse me,' Ash said, 'I'm looking for…'But the girl interrupted him with the sweetest smile quite at odds with her sinister appearance.

'The stables? Floster's? It's up the top road to the right out of town. You can't miss it.' Again Ash was surprised for she spoke with the most pukka of accents which belied her appearance.

'Er, no actually. I'm looking for the village of Dalton in Droverdale.'

She raised an eyebrow, cocking her head to one side with surprise.

'You're not here for the horses then?

'No, an art exhibition,' he said and could scarcely believe it himself.

At the top of the hill outside the village a group of about fifteen race horses descended lazily from their gallop on the moors. The young stable boys and girls riding them jockey style were relaxed, stirrups down, chatting to each other and on their mobile phones. Ash slowed down to let them pass, watching in amazement the raw power of the beautiful animals; multi-millions of pounds worth of stock just clip clopping along a public road. The young people gave him a wave of thanks as they passed. Quite a few of the jockeys were of Indian, Asian or perhaps even South American origin. No wonder no one had given him a second glance at the newsagent's.

When the last horse had passed, Ash accelerated up the hill. After the traffic clogged freeways of Dubai the lure of an open road was joy. He'd always loved narrow English country roads; how they curved and twisted, nursing the lie of the land, how they had stories to tell, a thousand years of hooves and travellers' footprints.

The gallop ran across the open moor with the road parallel to it for a short distance. What a riot of colour! It was impossible to put a name to such variety. The heather, was it purple, violet, burgundy, perhaps maroon? The bracken, brown, auburn or was it rust, wine, red, copper even gold? And the green, oh the greens! After years in a desert city, he marvelled at the shifting seas of green. Surely there must be more words in English for green than green? Emeralds, khakis, pea greens, sea greens, leaf greens, olive greens, they merged, diluted, concentrated, formed and reformed with the autumn light. And then quite unexpectedly he was descending into Droverdale. The Dale revealed itself coyly from the top of the moor; soft curvaceous hills, the two sides, one in darkness, one in light, disappearing into distant mountains that were smudges of green, purple and black. The car went down and the Dale took him in, guiding him between dry stone walls down into a deep dell, dark with trees and then out again into flashing sunlight.

The village of Dalton was made up of two lines of light coloured Yorkshire stone houses on either side of the main street which followed the path of a stream. It ran along the side of the Dale for about half a mile, ascending gently. Remembering Isa's directions, Ash drove past the pub, the Georgian house with the two large trees on either side of the gate, the village hall, the shabby looking milking parlour, the austere façade of the Methodist Chapel and the garage, which on that afternoon, had two farm boys chatting astride quad bikes outside.

Isa had told him that their old farmhouse would be out of the village up the track to the right in a small spur valley. As

Ash passed the signs for *Top Farm* and *Top Farm House*, he felt his heart skip a beat. *Top Farm House* was Isa's place. What folly, what delusion, what impulse had brought him here to this mysterious, secret place? What was he expecting to find? He did not rightly know, except that he had come.

Winding down the window, he drove slowly up the single track road, passing *Top Farm* where a dog barked enthusiastically from behind the gate. Still no sight of Isa's place. On he drove until he thought he might fall off the end of the world. Doubting himself, fearing that he might once again be lost, he parked the car and continued on foot. The wind tugged gently at his hair. A chorus of sheep bleated in the fields and to his right a little mountain stream gurgled down from the hills. At just after 3.30 pm, the late autumn sun was failing fast, chasing him and the colours, herding them in for the night. He puffed to the top of a crest in the road, and all of a sudden, there was Top Farm House. It nestled amongst a copse of trees in a fold of the land, its back windowless to the north against the wind and weather. And then he saw her too, Isabella Angus, the woman he had travelled half way around the world to find.

She was sitting like a milk maid on a large disused concrete delivery stone at the side of the road, still, so still, looking out across to the rocky outcrops on the far side of the valley. The breeze, softer in the lea of the land, played at her golden hair. He just stood there, staring and it seemed to him that at that moment she was the centre of the glory of the day. She did not move, her pale oval face serene in the late afternoon sunshine. She was wearing a green waxed jacket, red skirt and dark green wellington boots which hung heavily down the high sided delivery stone as if worn by a child. And Ash did not move, unwilling to disturb her peace. But she must have sensed him, suddenly looking up, shading her eyes against the glare of the sun. And the spell was broken.

'Isabella, well, hi there!' He heard his voice squeak and saw her jump, recoil a little with surprise, or was it fear? He could have kicked himself. But the incompetent words were already out of his mouth and he was half-running, half-walking towards her.

He watched, as if in slow motion, she eased herself down from the delivery stone, smoothing down her skirt with her hands, the same old nervous habit she had had as a young woman. Then he had her in his arms and for a second she yielded, warm and soft, smelling of lemons, a hint of wood smoke overlaid with fresh air and sunshine. Gently, firmly, she put her palm on his chest keeping him at distance, offering him instead courteously but formally, one cheek then the other.

Chapter 20

'I'm sorry I'm late. Getting out of London was a nightmare.' Ash apologised.

'Oh, don't worry about that. It's just lovely to see you.' Isa hesitated. They both did, smiling awkwardly like teenagers, looking at each other then looking away. Isabella took a deep breath and brushed her skirt again. 'I tried to book you into the Woodcutter's Arms but I'm afraid they only have four rooms. With my agent and a couple of reviewers up from London, they were full.' She tidied a curl behind her ear. 'I've put you in the stables instead.'

'Baby Jesus, is it? No room at the inn!' He quipped.

'Don't worry! You're not sleeping with the ox and the ass.' There was intimacy in their humour which eased the tension just a little. She led him across a gravel yard about twenty yards from the main house to an old stable block that had been restored.

'We left it a ramshackle play den for the twins when they were little but then we did it up. Let it out to friends of friends. Holiday cottage, that sort of thing.' She talked in a friendly but business-like manner as if running through a check-list in her head. Welcoming guests to the Stables was clearly a well-rehearsed routine. She was hiding behind formality and politeness. He knew it and so did she.

'I've given you our newly re-fitted upstairs studio apartment.' She handed him the key. 'Lovely views over the valley to Rolly Crags. Breakfast in the main house. How about eight-thirty? I think you'll find everything you need.'

'I'm sure I'll be just fine.' He held her gaze for a few seconds, trying to read the frown lines between her brows and the tiny wrinkles round her eyes that scrunched up when she laughed. But she looked at him with an air of caution and puzzlement as if he were someone she half-recognised but could not quite place.

'I thought we might go for tea in Croughburn before the exhibition.' She hurried on, looking away. 'It starts a five-thirty and supper will be late. Something to keep us going? Perhaps you might like to get your bag from the car and freshen up? See you in the yard in twenty minutes.'

They sat on chintz cushions facing each other in the window seat of a tea shop in Croughburn. The wall opposite them was decorated most incongruously with an idealised mural of what Ash supposed to be rural Tuscany. It suggested to customers that they might be sitting on the balcony of a grand villa watching the sunset over the olive groves. He thought about how Isa had driven them both at what had felt like break-neck speed in her bone breaker of an ex-British Army Land Rover, over the top of Droverdale and down a precipitous road into the next, much larger dale. And now there she was, sitting opposite him, daintily pouring the tea. Every movement she made was measured, controlled, too controlled, her hands and wrists graceful with the teacups, plates and saucers.

'You haven't changed a bit,' he said, and he meant it. If her cheeks had fallen in a tad and her skin puckered a little around her lips, such imperfections fascinated him. He wanted to know all the stories that had made them, to reach out and touch them, to smooth them away with kisses.

'Neither have you,' she wrinkled up her nose in that teasing way of hers and they both laughed at the absurdity of the notion that neither of them had changed.

'I thought you might have gotten fat.' He joked, for banter was easiest. It avoided the awkward questions.

'I thought you might have gone bald!' And then quick as a flash her guard was up again, her face shutting down, still formal, friendly but polite. 'Would you like a scone? Jam and cream? Do help yourself.' For a short time the tea did the talking, gurgling steaming into cups out of the flowered china teapot. The ritual of milk and sugar.

'Still two spoonfuls she asked.

'You remember?

'Of course.' She pushed the little pots of jam and cream his way.

He asked about Tony and the twins. She responded carefully, tactfully, as if placing her feet on slippery stepping stones, aware of the swirling currents that might sweep them both away. Jamie was an analyst, a scientist and Ferdie was turning out quite the opposite, more the poetic arty creative type. Ash felt like he was listening to the preamble to an up-beat annual report.

'Still playing cricket?' She asked in her turn.

He shook his head sadly.

'What a shame! You loved that game.'

'Too busy I guess. The pressure of work and the heat in

Dubai. But I'm quite fit; swim every day, golf once a week.'

'Golf! Seriously?'

'Yup, afraid so. Though I never really got into it like some guys. They're obsessed with the sport. For me it was always more for networking purposes and getting out of the office into the fresh air.'

Isa supped her tea then poured herself another cup, smoothed down her skirt and tidied again the cheeky curl back behind her ear.

'So what happened with your marriage?' she asked with false nonchalance. 'You didn't really explain on the phone.'

'Oh that!' He shrugged. 'It was quite farcical, looking back now. She turned out to be gay!'

Isa snorted, choking a little on her tea, not because Ash's ex-wife was a lesbian but because the possibility of it had never occurred to her.

'Sex was lousy right from the start. Truth was she was far too clever for me, quite brilliant actually. We struggled on for about eighteen months for the sake of the families. The wedding itself cost a fortune and that's not to mention all the gold jewellery. Then one day, cool as a cucumber, a few days after her younger sister was safely married and returned from honeymoon, Ritu announced that she was moving to New York with her girl-friend from college. She'd got a job at the UN. He raised his hands to the ceiling. 'And that was that. I kinda gave up on marriage after that,' he grinned and shrugged his shoulders.

But Isa looked right into him, unnerving him with her bright blue eyes and he was ashamed. She had always seen through of him, right to the heart of the most unspeakable things, she seemed to know without knowing. Perhaps that was why he had sought her out.

CHAPTER TWENTY ONE

Ash was not sure what he had been expecting at Isabella's exhibition, pretty little paintings in a damp village hall perhaps? Instead, he found himself in a brand new colonnaded fine arts and auction house on the outskirts of Croughburn where Isabella's stunning landscapes adorned the walls of a large marble exhibition hall.

He was standing with the Goth girl from the newsagent's in front of a large three panelled painting. She was, it turned out, also an artist. Her name was Lucinda and she had dressed up for the occasion in a long purple dress, her hair rolled up dramatically at the front and pinned with a silver-eyed black dragon.

Waterfall at Hooting Hole in Spring, the caption next to the painting informed the viewer.

'I didn't expect the paintings to be so large.' Ash confided, standing back a little to better admire the glorious cascade of colours: blues, greens, yellows, flying droplets of silver. 'It's so real. I can almost hear the roar of water, feel the spray on my face.'

'Isa is just so talented. The way she manipulates media, oils, acrylics, she works them all with such ease. Awesome!' The girl's eyes shone with delight. 'And she's humble too, generous and supportive of me and my work.' After a slow start the hall was filling up with guests clutching champagne glasses. Lucinda and Ash moved onto the next picture.

Top Hill in Winter

'Look how she uses the light, discovers the colour, even in this snow scene; the contrasts, the red of the berries, the purple in the grey, the hint of green in the black of the dry stone walls. Her work is so alive, nothing ever fixed, always moving. That's her magic'

Ash nodded, his head bursting with the sound of Isa playing Bach, his own voice weaving a soft response. As their conversation lapsed Ash looked over towards Isabella who was surrounded by a small crowd of people. She had discarded her muddy green wellies for a pair of elegant high heeled light tan shoes and had in fact been wearing a red shift dress under her waxed jacket. The dress was now adorned simply with a tiny pearl on a gold chain at the V-neck. She looked beautiful as she smiled, shook hands, kissed and hugged her guests. Many of them, it was clear, were friends from the village enjoying a Friday night out. They were an odd assortment; farmers in tweeds, jumpers and ties, some of their wives wearing flowery dresses and smart jackets as if they were expecting a wedding or going to a day at the races, others still in wellies, overalls and anoraks, and one very elegant old dame with pearls at her neck pushing a walker with her handbag hanging from it. Some had come directly from work, a nurse in uniform holding the hands of two earnest little boys in red soccer kit, three bearded workmen, builders, painters or plumbers perhaps, who had left their boots at the door and padded round in stockinged feet, and a scrawny looking girl from the stables wearing grubby jodhpurs and a tatty old fleece. She was accompanied by a young man similarly attired with a wispy beard on his chin who looked Nepalese. All these people mixed with the critics, potential buyers and glamorous art professionals.

Then Isabella beckoned to Lucinda who excused herself. Her place at Ash's side was instantly taken by a young man in a purple velvet suit. He had had his eye on Ash all evening.

'Alexis Foster, Isabella's agent.' The handsome curly haired man in his early thirties had a firm confident handshake. 'You're from Dubai?'

'India actually but yes I live there. Isa and I are old friends.' Ash could predict the flow of the man's fishing trip before it had barely begun. General state of the market in Dubai, fine art opportunities, might he perhaps be buying?

'Alexis, I'm afraid art is not really my thing. There is a grow-ing art market in Dubai but much of it is Arabic, Persian or Indian in orientation and that was before the crash.' They pretended to sip champagne and made small talk watching the ebb and flow of the guests.

'She's brilliant, you know, Isabella. One of my best selling artists. We don't really need this show here but she insists on supporting the local community. Jolly good for her!' Alexis sighed conspiratorially as if to say, what can I do about it and offered Ash his business card, just in case.

'For sure her pieces might be difficult to label but they will prove great investments. Abstract, yes but I prefer intuitive. Before she came along Yorkshire Dales paintings were nothing more than insipid watercolours, but she's moved the whole scene on to the next level, bigger bolder, vibrant colour. My buyers love her work, especially the corporates. She's still sell-ing despite the crash. They want something dramatic and contemporary for large London houses, New York apartments and yachts. And I know she's not giving me everything.' He tapped his nose. 'She can't fool me. She's on the cusp of something else. I feel it in my bones! The way she interprets the hills is so sensual, spiritual, erotic even, it's coming full circle, almost figurative. She's got some more canvases hidden away up there at the farm house.'

'Thank God that's over!' Isabella kicked off her high heels and turned to warm the soles of her feet on the great tank of an oven in the corner of her kitchen. 'I love being an artist but hate the selling and sucking up side of things. It's so pretentious.'

It was well after ten before supper at the pub had finished and the night brought with it a stiff winter chill.

'Pffff,' she rolled her shoulders and pushed back her hair from her face. As she did so, her face relaxed, opening up, losing some of the lines.

'I think it was a lovely occasion. You're blessed to have so many friends.' Ash said.

She nodded.

'Funny how this village has become my home, the dales such an inspiration. I wasn't that keen when Tony first inherited the place and now it's I who wants to spend time here, not him.' She paused, embarrassed, before hurrying on. 'Want a drink; tea, coffee, whisky brandy, cocoa?'

'Cocoa would be great. I've not had a hot chocolate for years.' He sat down at the kitchen table watching her fetch the milk from the fridge, pour two cupfuls into the saucepan and heat it up on top of the massive Aga.

'Remember College food? Funny, what I miss about England; baked beans, jam roly-poly and custard, treacle sponge and spotted dick!' He licked his lips and they both laughed, the years, the differences, suddenly collapsing between them so that they were almost young again.

'I don't think we got off to a very good start this afternoon,' he said.

She shrugged, her back to him, standing at the Aga.

'You seemed so American. The way you talk has changed. It gave me a shock.'

'Really?'

The milk began to boil and Isa decanted it into two mugs, stirring in the cocoa powder.

'You used to speak with the quaintest 1930's style Indian English.

'Too long in Dubai I guess. We Indians are a strange bunch. We chuck out you Brits and within one generation we're speaking American!" He exaggerated a drawl, laughing at himself. 'Pax Britannica followed by Pax Americana!'

The chair scrapped on the tiled floor as Isa sat down opposite him and the two of them sat warming their hands on the steaming mugs.

'Well, if I've gone American, you've cut your hair!' Then quickly added, 'It suits you,' lest she thought it a criticism.

'Long hair proved rather impractical after the twins were born. They were always pulling it or it was getting messed up with baby food.'

'It can't have been easy, caring for two babies at once?'

'Let's say it wasn't the happiest time of my life.'

They sipped their cocoa listening to an owl hooting outside.

'Do you miss Tony? I mean he's away so much.' Ash went on gently.

'Not really.' Isabella said quickly looking down at her mug. 'We get on better like this. He has his life and I have mine. We come together around the boys.'

Ash pursed his lips. The owl fell quiet, leaving the silence between them.

'Don't you worry that he might have someone else?' Ash probed after a while.

'I've decided not to' she replied simply. 'A glass half-full is better than one half-empty.'

He nodded, accepting the coded confession of her loneliness in the spirit that it had been given and was surprised to recognise in it a reflection of his own.

'He's flying back on the Sunday night flight and I will drive back to Birmingham on Monday,' she added in that matter of fact way of hers.

Then suddenly without warning, it slipped out.

'I was made redundant.' There, Ash had said it, loudly, clearly, painlessly. It was so easy with Isabella, it always had been. With her he could be himself. 'Several months ago now,' he clarified.

'Oh no! Why didn't you tell me?'

'Not much point. Nothing to worry about. I've got money. If I never work again in my life, I'll be more than fine.'

She shifted uneasily in her chair and looked unconvinced. 'What will you do?'

He shrugged. 'Look for another job, maybe start my own business. I'm getting too old and expensive to hire.'

'What about going home, to India?'

He shook his head.

'Isabella, I am Indian. It is who I am, who I shall always be, but I can't go back.' He sighed. 'God has been very generous, more than generous. But I don't deserve a cent of it. I've played hard, played rough, not always been too clean. Enough was never enough for me. I always wanted more.'

'I am sure that you worked very hard and achieved a great deal.' Isa soothed.

Suddenly desperate, he looked to into her large, kind eyes as if they might save him from what was coming next. But already his mind had slipped a gear and there was nothing he could do to stop it. It was re-running the past, a horror that had always returned unrequested over the years, a terrible thing that haunted, tormented and terrified him.

'Help! Help!'

He was pulling at the policeman's arm.

'Please God, you've got to help!' The smell of smoke, caustic fire, burning, manufactured flames. The crowd dancing, jigging, whirling, chanting.

Khoon Ka Balda Khoon. (Blood for Blood)

'No!' He banged his fist on the table and she pushed back her chair in alarm.

'The truth is that is none of my wealth or so called success is mine. By rights it should belong to someone else, my best friend, my brother. My whole adult life, I have lived in a dead man's shoes. I am an imposter, a fraud, a trumped up trickster who got too big for his boots.

Ash then spoke almost in a whisper so that Isabella had to lean forward to hear him, the only other sounds, the quiet hum of the Aga and the haunting, piercing crying of a fox.

'When a big tree falls the earth shakes. 1984, the year Prime Minister Indira Gandhi was assassinated, the year before we met.'

Isabella nodded in acknowledgement.

'I remember Mark Tully's reports on the BBC.'

'Yes. On the morning of the 31st October our Prime Minister was gunned down by her Sikh bodyguards. My life changed for ever in the days that followed. My comfortable privileged world fell apart.' He opened his hands, but in his mind they were running deep red with blood. 'It's a terrible thing when your country betrays you and you lose faith in all that you had been brought up to believe in; modern, secular, democratic, India.'

Again the fox wailed, bitter, harsh, haunting in the night. Ash felt himself start to tremor and quake inside and held on firmly to the cup of cocoa to steady himself. He wanted to reach out and stroke Isabella's hair as if that too would give him courage. Some of her golden curls had fallen in a tangle round her earnest face. He had kept silent for so long but now the pent up feelings and emotions were choking in his chest and throat, struggling to form words. Taking a deep breath, he stared at Isabella's face, focusing on the softness in her clear blue eyes. She did not look away.

'I had a friend, Shiv, Shivraj Singh. I think I told you about him?'

Again Isa nodded.

'You were at boarding school together. You used to brush his hair; beautiful long black shiny hair.'

'Isa you have a memory like an elephant!' Ash managed a grin.

'Yes, Shiv was Sikh, never cut his hair. I was a Hindu but it never mattered a jot. We went all the way through school and College together. He was my brother, my best friend in the world.' Ash swallowed hard to control shaking, sipping on his cocoa.

'The morning Mrs Gandhi was assassinated Shiv and I had been at nets. Cricket crazy dudes we were back then! We didn't hear about it until lunch at College. There was one TV for the whole place in the common room and we all crowded in to hear the news, transistor radios blaring at the same time. They'd taken Mrs Gandhi to the top hospital. First they announced that she was dead and later that it was her Sikh bodyguards who had murdered her. We knew then that there would be trouble. Shiv wanted to go home right then to look after his parents and sisters who lived in an affluent suburb of Delhi, but I persuaded him to wait until the morning when things would have calmed down on the streets.' Ash stopped, itching, tingling, the blood rushing first to his head then to his feet, that smell, that terrifying burning stench that had clung to him all his adult life, burning flesh, bodies reduced to bone.

'The next day we slept in. Classes had been cancelled. We were so naïve! At last Shiv was all ready to set out and I insisted on accompanying him part of the way for safety's sake.

'"No need, Bhai." He put his arm round my shoulders. "Who is going to mess with me!" And he was quite right. At six foot eight inches in his turban, one look from him and trouble always walked away. All the same I went with him and we took the bus. It was a beautiful autumn day, warm but not hot, so benign. It wasn't until we were approaching Connaught Circus that we saw the smoke rising in great black columns into the blue sky and then the marauding crowds of men. They were stopping buses and cars, pulling people out. The old lady in the seat in front of us was quickest off the mark. I guess she had seen these horrors before.

'"They're looking for sardars." She turned to Shiv and me. "Quick, hide under the seat." But the idea was quite ridiculous. How was such a giant of a man going to hide under a low bus seat and anyway, we were young and privileged, insulated from the brutalities of real life. Hiding wasn't in our nature.' Again Ash was forced to stop, his throat burning dry, blinking fast trying to slow the visions leaping in front his eyes. He was somewhere else now, barely present in Isa's farmhouse kitchen.

'They piled on thick and fast, onto the bus. I don't remember much. Fists, punches, kicking, swearing, the smell of them, feral, of sweat, oil, cigarettes, stale cooking, and cheap after shave. They had us both off the bus and were dragging Shivraj down. He fought, like a tiger and I did too, trying to defend him.

'"Leave him," Shiv was shouting in my defence. "He's a Hindu. Come on scum! Want a fight?" The mobs were like wild dogs. They ripped off his turban and had him by the hair, trying to cut it with a pair of garden shears. Shiv was having none of it. My God, he fought. Such strength, such courage, such a beautiful young man!' Ash paused and closed his eyes to control the nightmare before continuing.

'But they were too many for us. They already had beaten four or five other Sikh men senseless. Then I saw them coming with the cans, full of petrol, kerosene and a big metal tub with what looked like code numbers on. They were pulling out the stoppers getting ready to douse their victims. "Wanna burn too boy, burn with the stinking traitor Sikhs? *Khoon Ka Balda Khoon! Khoon Ka Balda Khoon! Khoon Ka Balda Khoon!*'

Ash stopped with his hands over his ears, the faces of the men in the crowd leaping before him, the thin young man with a sprawling red birth mark the shape of south America on his right chin, the older man, wiping Shiv's blood gleefully over his face as if anointing himself for war.

That's when I ran. "I'll be back Bhai, hang on. I'll fetch the police." I was frantic, running like the wind, shouting, screaming. "Help! Help! They're burning my friend. Call the police!" I hadn't gone far, just rounding corner, it was as quiet as early Sunday morning. The police were just standing there in the shadow of the colonnades staring at the pigeons. I begged, I implored, I threatened to tell all the politicians and big wigs I could think of, but they turned away, looking down over their moustaches as if I were a cockroach they could crush with a lazy stamp of a booted foot.'

Ash's voice gave out with the effort of recollection. Reaching out across the table top, Isa took his hands in hers. Small hands, warm hands, rough artist's hands. Ash felt himself sag.

'I went back and back for days,' his voice cracked and he wasn't speaking American any longer. 'Together with another lad from the cricket team, his Dad lent us his car and driver. We rescued one Sikh family from their home, hid the father and elder child in the boot, the mother and the baby under our feet in the back seat and managed to get them to one of the refugee camps that were springing up. But we never found Shiv.' The fox was silent now, the owl too, only the Aga hummed.

'On the fifth day after Mrs Gandhi's assassination, I heard that some bodies had been found in a lock-up garage not far from where Shiv had been taken. When I got there the police were already clearing away the corpses, burnt so badly, faceless.

Again Ash stopped, his head in his hands, blood booming like cannons in his ears so that he feared he might faint. 'I can't begin to describe it. Skin, muscle, faces, people stripped white to bare bone. What was it, what manner of burning could do that to human beings? But one man, one huge skeleton, still had some of his beautiful long hair.' He felt Isa holding his hands, calmly in hers, the steady pulse of her entering him.

'It wasn't your fault. You did all you could.' But he raised a hand to stop her, he had not finished.

'Recently I read something on the Internet that said that elements within the Congress government had supplied military grade white phosphorus to the thugs doing their dirty work. He stopped, consumed by a rage so violent it made him shake almost to the point of throwing up. But still there was still more. Now he had started he wanted her to know everything, the whole story, one he had never told a living soul.

'There were two India Scholarships to Oxford that year. Shiv and I had both applied. Shiv had been awarded one, the other going to another student. Don't you see?'

But she did not.

'Isa, it was never meant to be me. After Shiv died, they gave his scholarship to me. His murder gave me the golden ticket, the chance to escape India and ultimately become an investment banker and live the gilded life I have enjoyed. But I never could hope to match up to him, to be half the man he would have been. He was extraordinary. I am mediocre at best.'

They sat for a long time in silence, Isa still holding his trembling hand, patting it gently as if he were a child.

'You're so kind,' he said at last.

'No,' she shook her head. 'I'm not. If I were, I would not

have invited you here.'

A spiralling sense of falling, Ash with a gasp hauling himself out of pitch black, he didn't know where. He groped with the palm of his hand for the pillow next to him. It was empty. Where was he? India? No car horns, voices, shouts and incessant background hullabaloo that even gated compounds and double glazing could never quite cut out. Dubai? No hum of air conditioner that he always left on low even when he did not need it. Slowly his mind came together in the form of Isabella driving the Land Rover the previous night; lights on beam, up the bumpy dirt track to the cottage, her gloved hand changing down gears at his side. The gears had grated a little as she put her foot down to manage a muddy gradient in the road. Most of the women in his world were either driven by chauffeurs, or if they did drive, they complained furiously about it, as if they were too good for such a menial chore. He sat up in bed and reached for his phone. Five-seventeen am. Damn jet lag! He was getting old. Turning on his right side he pulled the duvet over his head and scrunched his knees up to his chest; an ancient position of warmth and comfort he had discovered as an eleven year old on the first night in his bunk at boarding school. Putting his nose to his knees, he breathed in the warmth of his body. But sleep was proving hard to get and it refused to let him make up the deficit hours.

Sighing, he threw back the duvet and once more picked up his phone. Loyal technology blue at his touch, it promised instant company, but the icons were dead under his finger print.

'No signal here. It's the hills.' He saw the tiny tips of Isabella's slightly crooked bottom teeth in her half smile, and her characteristic gesture of upturned white palms, 'That is why I like Droverdale. No one can get me!'

It was quiet, too quiet, only the tinkling of the hillside stream. Ash was afraid of being still.

'Damn!' He got up. It was cold, just as Isabella had warned, a musty chill with the beginning of a winter bite, which reminded him of the Delhi of his childhood. He loped over to the window and drew the curtains. On the far side of the valley, the gaunt blacker than black outline of Rolly Crags lay like abandoned dinosaur teeth bared along the top of the moor; ice cut, stone wrecked, the debris of a prehistoric life.

Perching on the windowsill, he tugged at the old fashioned window catches. There were two, one long arm at the bottom and a catch half way up. He had not seen a design like that since he had left Oxford. Surprising him, the window offered no resistance and he leant out. He remembered that the old stables had been left initially as a children's den and in his mind's eye saw two blond haired boys launching paper aeroplanes down into the garden on a summer day. But now the first frost was there. Forgivingly, it nipped at his cheeks and lips inducing a gasp. Cherishing the cold, he held the air as long he could in the top of his chest, releasing it slowly into the blackness. Putting his elbow on the windowsill he stuck out his tongue, licking the moisture from the air. He was no longer afraid, cradled in this mountain womb. The only sounds were the beating of his heart and the bleating of a ghost of a sheep in the shadows beyond the gurgling stream that knew no drought. He shivered.

'Man, it's cold!' Crossing the room he swaddled himself in a dressing gown. It bore the fragrance of lavender which returned him to summer. He felt again a shower of weakness, the same sensation he had experienced when hearing Isabella's voice on the phone just a few days ago. Lifting the latch to the door at the top of the stairs he went down and out into the darkness. As he crossed the yard the security light clicked on and he unlocked the door to the main house, entering the hall. He removed his shoes, the oak floor acknowledging his weight with a creak like an aged knee joint. Moving along the passage, he hesitated briefly at the kitchen door then opened it and went in. In the gloom, the squat cream curved Aga enticed from the far wall, humming its gentle lullaby, promising warm embrace. Cautiously, Ash approached it, as a pilgrim to a shrine. Bowing his head, he reached out his hands turning his palms up and down, playing with the thermals over the huge round hot plates.

'What? Don't you look at me like that?' He squared up to the cheeky sheep in the picture made of coloured tiles that decorated the space above the oven. The fat orange kettle squatting on the warming plate shared the joke almost winking.

'Come on, clever clogs! I dare you! Make me some tea!' He smiled to himself. How come such a billion dollar deal maker as himself was terrified of an old oven? And anyway the kettle would whistle and wake up Isabella. The thought of her sleeping upstairs so near to him after all these years, was magic; her hair feathering over the pillow, the beat of her heart and her sweet breath. He did not want to do anything that might break the spell. Turning his back to the Aga, he raised his feet one by one as if for blessing, placing them flat against the lower oven doors for warmth. The Aga seemed to hum more loudly and through the window the stars retreated into the grey of early dawn. Then he saw it; a low door in the far right hand corner of the kitchen had been left ajar.

Who was this girl, this woman, Isabella? He crossed the kitchen and pushed open the door. He found himself in an orangery with floor to ceiling windows overlooking the Dale. White sheeted shapes, strange faces, boxes with triangular corners, a tatty old chaise longue, emerged from the half-light. In the far corner by the window, he saw the shadow of an easel with a huge picture on it, next to it a table with heaps of brushes and paints. Strange, for in the rest of the house everything had its place, but here there was disorder.

Alone in the centre of room, he watched the pink dawn rise over Rolly Crags curdling the mist into wispy breaths which drifted like brush strokes to paint tenderness into the day. The ancient stones softened almost to a smile, and charcoal lines tamed fields out on the moor. The sun swelled papaya, ripening, mixing with mango, red, copper and gold, until the sunshine came, and tweaked the raindrops on the trees into pearls. Sunlight streamed into the room and Ash felt as if he were standing under a spinning crystal dome in a holy place. Rainbow butterflies played about, swelling into a kaleidoscope of colours, green turning to heliotrope, smudging purple into ink and hazing out again through sky blue oceans. And all around were the visions of far flung places that were Isabella's paintings. He saw a beach and sea, the bronze and blue evaporated almost to a white haze, the spray from the white crested waves rising like mist in the air melding sea and shore. In the foreground was the grey shadow of a man holding a camel on a lead, its red harness with golden bells jarring the sunlight. Ash remembered it as a place from his own childhood, but he could not think where.

Hanging next to the beach scene was another painting, wild circles of colour, women dancing in a castle courtyard. Their full skirts, scarlet, yellow and fuchsia pink with black spots spinning out wide, the colours vivid, against a golden evening light, faster and faster they turned, the spots smudging almost into lines until the women at the outside seemed in danger of spinning off the edge. Bewitched, he looked at another smaller oil, a lone woman, her hair in a tight black bun, reaching out her arms, dancing with her shadow in the lamplight. The pictures were all oils, the colours and brush strokes thicker and heavier, occasionally jerky and crude, as if Isabella could not keep up with her ideas and had lost patience. But it was the seeming imperfection that made everything right. Ash stared. This was what the agent in the purple velvet pants had been talking about; talent, highly marketable. He began lifting dust sheets. He could not help himself: mirages of gardens, green beyond green with mangoes and lemons, hibiscus and rose, waterfalls and peacocks, crevices and caves and wild white seas. But then there was something else, a stack of wild pencil sketches of a naked man and a woman entwined. At first the models were young, their muscles taught and smooth, air brushed visions of a brown man with a white woman. In some the figures were equal in size, in others the man smaller, the woman bigger, heads and limbs twisted this way and that, sometimes an agony of distortion as if almost broken. There were studies of their faces; the man, clean shaven, then with a beard, the woman wrinkled and old, then smooth, peach-like, young. The papers rustled in his hands, until he came across one with an old man and an old woman in an embrace. This time the composition was wrong, skewing the whole picture off to one side and Isabella had crossed it out with two decisive, unruled pencil lines. He began looking for the paintings, for he knew this was just the beginning and there would be more. Under a dust sheet on the far side of the room behind her easel, bending awkwardly, he found them. He held his breath. There were three oils on the same theme, two half-finished and one half-begun, a brown man wrapped around a white woman half-lying, half-sitting, ying and yang, on a bed in the shadow of fire light. Standing up, shading his eyes against the low sun, Ash looked at the huge picture on the easel. A vibrant autumn landscape at first inspection, it took his breath away; henna, ochre, soft curves, undulating light and clouds, a cleft that might be a river running below and yet the picture was alive. The most sensual painting he had ever seen, the form, shape and colour might be of a landscape but subtly it was of two people lying together. The woman's head in the shape of a hill resting on the shadowy rise opposite that suggested a chest, serene cliff eyes half closed, looking down, her sunny light leg reaching over his right, around and up his purple green back. Her left arm was folded into the curve of her breasts against the illusion of hairs of his chest, trees. Part of her soft cloudy form cradled the rocky back of his head, the tresses of her silver hair falling as the river from the nape of her neck. It wrapped around the shadow spur of his arm binding them together.

Abstract, figurative, intuitive. Ash did not have the vocabulary to describe what he saw, but he understood the scale and ambition of the piece. Another person looking at the painting might have seen something else, but all this is what Ash saw in Isabella's vision of the land. How had she managed it? And yet he felt that there was something not quite right about it, as if it were almost done but had not quite complete. The light perhaps was a little flat? He noted the patches where the paint had been removed and other parts where Isa was in the process of reworking the landscape of the bodies, crevices and hills, shadow and shade, light and dark. Reaching out his index finger until it almost touched the canvas, he traced the narrow lane that defined the contours of woman's left leg and the man's hip until their skins merged into shadow.

In the distance, a sheep bleated. He tried to look away from the picture, but the sunlight now beginning to stream through the windows momentarily blinded him. The door creaked. He knew she was there although he could not see her. The shadow of her stepped out into the centre of the room. Like him, she was wrapped in a white towelling dressing gown. He saw for the first time that she too was getting old, the line of skin that was the beginning of a sagging chin, her legs thin and pale, her toes like tiny claws. She pushed her pillow dishevelled fringe back from her face and he saw where it had been dyed.

'I see you have found me. This is me. The dream of all of me.'

'I know,' His words came heavy, as if drawn in a wooden bucket from the bottom of a deep well. Stepping from behind the easel, he put his arm out to draw her to him. She gasped with pain, relief, desire.

'I am sorry,' he said but then there were no more words. Instead, he stroked her hair, teasing it, combing it gently with his fingers just as he had done all those years ago.

'Don't be!' At last she lifted her head, heavy still with sleep, eyes as if drugged, her mouth begging like a little bird. She was like water in his arms and he gripped her tightly afraid she would flow away between his fingers.

'Catch me! I am falling.' Her tears were warm on his cheeks and she gripped the collar of his dressing gown.

'I know,' he managed to say again. 'Please don't cry.' He caught a tear with the tip of his index finger and put in his mouth, kissing her. She pulled his head back down to her and the strength rushed out of him, as she infused him with her softness. In the distance an unlikely bird began to sing, sad and slow, spider-like, spinning fresh threads of a morning raag from the night that was gone. It sang like a novice, running away with itself so that the melody snapped in places and needed to start again.

'I think you have an Indian bird in your garden,' Ash whispered, eyes closed, swaying a little with her in his arms

'Yes and he is singing in the autumn just for us. Time for breakfast!' she stroked his face, but her eyes were red.

'You haven't changed!' He smiled. 'Still that mix of passion and pragmatism I love so much.' And the word he had avoided all these years was said.

The kitchen was warm, the morning sunshine firing the oak cupboards to saffron bronze. With the tip of his finger Ash traced a curl in a knot of wood on the kitchen table then watched her bending down to a cupboard next to the Aga.

'Pancakes!' She clattered about amongst the pots and pans, hauling out a huge cast iron frying pan. 'I promised that I'd test that golf course fitness of yours on some Yorkshire hills. Pancakes will set us up for the day. Stretching on tip toes, she reached for a packet of flour from a cupboard on the other side of the Aga. The cupboard was jammed to bursting. A small pot of something fell out and she caught it with her left hand.

'Well held!' He joked, and realised that the house was an illusion of organisation.

'Well, don't just stand there! Eggs are in the fridge.' She gestured to the corner of the kitchen.

'You remember the small things, like my sweet tooth' He handed her the box of eggs.

'Get a cup and crack them for me. Two will do.'

'I have no idea the last time I did this,' he said beating the eggs and the flour.

The oil sizzled in the pan as he dropped the mixture in, watching it flood to the sides and slowly turn yellow to gold.

'Here goes!' he grinned, flipping the first pancake with a spatula. It tore slightly in the middle. 'Damn. But not bad for a first attempt, even if I say so myself!'

'Honey and lemon, or ham and cheese?'

'Do I need to answer that?'

She was making sandwiches and chopping an apple. 'It's from the garden.' She pointed to the tree through the window.

He watched her out of the corner of his eye as she laid the table. She was completely herself. There was a wisdom and an earthiness in her he could not find in younger women. She was not trying to be like the women in Dubai with their Facebook pages, blogs and parties, always organising, doing, announcing, seeing, being seen. And she did not seem to want anything from him. He could not remember feeling so at peace. Perhaps the last time was the final summer he had spent with his nanny, Pooja, before she had been dispatched back to Gujarat, and he had been put on the train in the middle of the night to go to boarding school.

The kettle whistled and Isa made the tea, pouring hers first, leaving his to stew in the pot on the warming plate. She had remembered he liked it strong. He carried the pancakes over to the table and sat down. She reached up, over him, to open a fly window and he put his hands on her breasts, bowing his head and burying it in the warmth and musk of her. She did not object and laid her hands on the top of his head, kissing his crown.

'I am counting the grey hairs.' Her voice was muffled and he pulled her onto his lap, letting her cover his face in kisses.

Through the open window the bird song grew faster, more insistent. Other birds were joining in.

'The pancakes!' She chided, tears falling again. 'They'll be getting cold. Eat!'

She spooned honey out of the pot, holding it high so it fell as liquid amber in circles on the pancake. She dotted the eyes and made the smiley mouth. He squeezed the lemon and fed her the first mouthful.

'Mmmmm! Not bad.' Her lips were sweet, wet and dripping with juice. He held her on his lap and she fed him as he fed her, off the same plate, until all was gone. Untangling herself without a word she went to fetch the teapot from the top of the Aga, treading carefully barefoot across the kitchen, as if marking each step from an ancient ritual dance. Sitting now on the far side of the table, she poured his tea.

'Tell me about the pictures,' he said.

She sighed.

'They're from my memory. Unlike the commercial pieces, with these experimental pieces I paint my dreams. Hubris perhaps, an attempt to leave something permanent behind for my children that one day they might understand. But they have their own lives to lead. The big seascape is something I remember from Pakistan, a beach I went to with my father once, it must have been Karachi. The gardens too, are something from Pakistan. And the dancers are from a fiesta in Jerez in Spain. And…,' she blushed.

'Everything about your painting tells me of a woman who craves colour,' he said. 'You seek it out in your work even in the dark winter days when the rest of us probably would not see it. Your dealer was right. You should sell these pieces. People would buy.'

She sipped her tea, looking away down the garden and Ash thought that he had irritated her again by mentioning money. She sighed.

'Sometimes I feel as if I am living with a blind man. My husband, he looks but does not see.' She pushed her hair back from her forehead and blew the steam from her cup. 'A deaf man, he listens but does not hear. Living with him is like every day trying to sound a gong which has no echo.' Again she sipped her tea, but looked straight up at Ash, searching, reading, plumbing the depths through his eyes.

'Tony is a good man, a good father. I married him. It is what I wanted at the time. Stability, certainty, Englishness! No more chasing round the world like my mother did with my father. I got what I wanted.'

Ash nodded. 'All husbands, perhaps are guilty of this. It is the nature of marriage, job, routine, providing.'

'That is why I come up here; to paint, to be myself. For a while, at least, to be free.'

He was dressed before she was and went down to the garden. Rosehips hung from a bush near the door like chillies drying in the sun on the veranda at his Aunt's house in Goa. The day had awoken to a riot of tumbledown colour, as if the festival of Holi had moved from spring to autumn and people had been throwing paint everywhere. The trees were of mustard, chutney and strawberry jam. He wandered down through the garden, following the whispers that told him he had been here before. Cobwebs draped in rows of dusty diamonds along the purple lavender to the side of the path and, high in the apple tree, the last fruit flaunted its seductive red. Around the base of the trunk a couple of crows mercilessly hollowed out the windfalls back to the skin. Nature was its own gardener here. There were no tenders and investment plans, musical fountains or sprinklers as in Dubai. The garden had its own life, its own design. Yet he had been here before, in this Yorkshire jungle, of that he was sure.

Hearing without knowing, he turned and saw a boy coming from the kitchen door. Shading his eyes against the sun, whistling a soft call, the lad scattered seed into the bird feeder, then turned and addressed Ash.

'Can you help me feed the sheep?' It was Isabella, in a flat cap, green jacket and wellington boots, striding down the path with a knife in her hand. She reached up, ruffled his hair, hesitated and kissed him.

'I look after the sheep when I'm up here, to help Stan out. He's the farmer at the bottom of the road. They used to be tenant farmers of the family and he still leases the field beyond the beck and the barn from us. The poor chap slipped a disc earlier this year and his wife has angina. He's a lot better now but it's a small thing just to keep an eye on the sheep. The grass is getting poor now and I want to put a little hay out for them. She led Ash to a small ramshackle barn below the house to the right that he had not noticed before. Remnants of honeysuckle still hung on in the shelter round the door. Winding a little around his finger, he rubbed the surviving flower and offered the scent to her. She smiled, inhaled then stood back to let him open the wooden door. He pressed his thumb into the heavy iron latch, it fitted exactly as if made for him. She went in first. He followed. It was warm and damp, full of old farm machinery, the air stale with time. He squinted up at the huge beam holding up the rafters.

'Droverdale is in a National Park and the barn is a listed building. We couldn't knock it down even if we wanted to. We English always look back, never forward. It is a blessing and a curse. ' Isabella shrugged and lifted a small bale of hay from the back wall of the barn.

'Here, let me help you,' Ash offered.

The bale hung between them by the string, cutting at their hands and they managed to drop it. Collapsing on it laughing, they sat arm in arm in semi-gloom watching the sunlight creep in through the gaps in the roof tiles and a field mouse scuttle in and out of a hole in the corner of the barn.

The sun was warm on their faces when they emerged from the barn, Ash refusing the wheelbarrow and carrying the bale for the sheep. At the end of the garden was a narrow bridge leading over the beck to the field. Two old trees had been twisted together to form a small arch on the near side of the bridge. Virginia creeper clung to the trees. Ash let Isabella pass onto the bridge first. Part of the creeper had fallen loose. Balancing the bale on the wooden side of the bridge, carefully he wound it back round the tree.

'My husband is always pulling that stuff off; says it will kill the trees.' The stream flashed up slices of silver through the cracks in the boards beneath their feet, and she was a ghost in the sunlight in his eyes.

'Perhaps it's the vine that holds the tree up?'

On the far side, Isabella lifted the latch to the small gate. The field opened before them, running down the hill to a dry stone wall, and beyond the red and gold tree line in the bottom of the dale.

'Here they are!' Seeing and hearing the couple approach, the sheep lifted their heads and came towards them. Isabella handed Ash the knife to cut the string around the bale.

'Here, like this.' She spread the hay on the ground. 'They don't really need much at this time of year, but even so.' Turning, without warning, she grabbed a ewe, expertly detaining it by the back of her head and checking it quickly as it continued to eat. 'Such daft things sheep. This one got caught in barbed wire in the spring. Tore at herself. The wound has been a devil to heal.'

She laughed, releasing the ewe with an affectionate slap on her back.

The jobs done, they set out on a walk. After the long haul flight Ash was keen for some fresh air. Isabella closed the gate to the yard, and turned out down the lane toward Stan's farm at the bottom of the hill.

'Where are we going?' He reached for her hand. As always at first, it was cold in his. Her answer was to slow her pace around his, the rhythm of his feet in his shiny new boots that he had bought in London. There was the soft chafing of his arms swinging in the raincoat she had lent him, and his breath, which he knew, came too eager and short. The smell of wood smoke drifted up from the early autumn fires in the village, reminding him of his father's cigarettes. They stopped short of the houses, cutting round the back of Stan's farm. The dogs barked from the front gate and the shadow of the back of a hand waved from a downstairs window. Isabella reached up her arm in acknowledgement. Her face was light and golden, innocent, like the day.

'Best not to go into the village.' She read his mind. 'It's a small community.'

They reached a gap in a dry stone wall closed with a small wooden gate, which tipped gently backwards downhill with the wall. It was just wide enough for one person to pass if they turned to the side. Deliberately, he blocked her way.

'How did you know?' she teased. 'These are called kiss gates in the Dales.' She looked round before pecking him on the cheek.

'I have been here before.' He grinned. 'In my past life.'

'Of course.' They walked due south across another field. At the next kiss gate between the fields Isabella blocked his way and exacted her toll. They startled a herd of cows in the field who abandoned their ruminating and lurched towards them, searching with old soul eyes.

'Hup, hup, hup,' Ash called, leading Isabella into the steaming midst of them, patting, pushing them gently on their mud encrusted rumps, talking to them in a language beyond time. They smelt of dung and rotting grass, and moo-ed and hustled gently against Ash in reply. The herd followed them almost to the gate at the bottom of the field, stopping short, as if hitting an invisible line, heeding an ancient call.

'They seem to know you? Isabella said. 'You have an old man's touch.'

'Of course they know me. I'm a good Hindu boy,' Ash shrugged. 'When I was a child, my grandmother used to give money to a goshala. It's kind of a cowshed for injured cows. The poor animals get hit by cars and trucks and get terribly injured on the roads in India. It's even worse these days with all the scooters. Sometimes my grandmother used to take me to visit the goshala. I suppose the language of cows is the same in all lands!'

They walked on blindly into the low autumn sun, not seeing where the field ended. When at last they reached a stile, Ash saw that it led to a narrow path down a hill into a thicket or small wood. They negotiated a way down the muddy path, until they came upon a stream. It tumbled and chattered down the hill beside them, dancing in and out of the trees, as might a small child, providing all the conversation. Down and down they went stepping on patches of sunlight that sneaked through the trees.

All of a sudden the stream rolled over the edge of a small ledge into a pool below. The path was steep, ground into stone and mud by the quiet passage of pilgrims. They slipped and slid their way down. She was nimbler than he but she let him guide her, reaching down for his hand, and he felt as if he were at was at the batsman's crease again, strong, steady and firm.

Down in the dell, water roared falling seemingly from the sky, splashing into a natural pool, spilling, splashing, soaking the rocks at their feet. From this pool the water flowed out into a lower, slightly larger pool and into a river that ran away down the Dale.

'The river Drover.' Isabella whispered, so as not to break the peace. 'And that is a small chapel.' She pointed to a ruin down by the river surrounded by trees, which rustled a quiet welcome.

'An ancient holy place,' Ash put his arm around Isabella's shoulder.

'In the early days of Christianity hermits lived here and then it was a chapel of ease for mass so that people did not need to walk all the way to the Abbey over at Wootondale, and later it became an inn.' She smiled. 'The English are very pragmatic!'

'There would be riots in India if a temple were turned into an inn!' Ash laughed.

She led him to the lower pool and they sat down on the stones around the edge. They were worn into seats by the passage of feet and hands. Isabella slipped off her coat, leaning against Ash, helping to remove his. Turning, he took off her hat and her hair was the sunshine in his day. The fall of the water had been broken in the upper pool and by the time it reached the lower pool it was a gentle trickle at the top so that the centre of the pool was almost mirror still.

Imperceptibly, the sun rose higher, marking time from their shadows in the pool. Reaching out his hand Ash caressed a patch of lichen growing on a stone behind. It was yellow and orange with spiky fronds like a sea anemone. Picking up a small pebble he threw it into the pool. It plopped, spreading concentric circles which gently faded away. He threw another and another making the flat stones jump and turn. Isabella joined in, copying him and the ripples met, playing off each other, reversing, and sending more and more out to the edges of the pool, until all was still. Standing up they sought out bigger stones, throwing them with great plonking splashes into the pool, watching the patterns of the waves, crash together, spread and lap up on shore. Kneeling, Ash untied Isabella's boots, tugging them off, caressing the tops of her feet. They were thin and white and her toe nails needed cutting. She bent down to him, in return, bowing and kissing his feet.

'Don't! I don't deserve it. 'Gently, he pulled her up gently, leading her into the shallows of the pool. The stones were sharp under their feet and they gasped with cold.

'It is not the Ganges,' she laughed.

'No and it's not Dubai. Here, is so much fresh water running free. It reminds me of holidays in Goa at my Aunt's house.'

He rolled up his shirt sleeves and paddled out, dipping his arms into the water to wash, reaching for her to follow. Cupping his hands he raised the water, letting it trickle as silver harp strings through his fingers. On the third scoop, he washed his face, scrubbing it red. Turning for her, he offered up the water for her to do the same.

He led her up the pool and over the rocks, toward the upper pool. Water pitter pattered around them as early raindrops until they were on a small shelf of mossy rock almost underneath the waterfall. The water crashed from a cleft above, splashing, the spray soaking them but they did not care. Unbuttoning his shirt, Ash stepped out to the edge of the rock, sticking his head under the current, gasping with cold, drinking from it, pulling her to him, the water gushing from his mouth.

The autumn sun touched the top of Rolly Crags. Walking through the ruins of the chapel, they spotted a break in the brambles by a fallen wall and sat down in the warmth. Above them the trees laid out a canopy of bronze, copper and gold. Isabella opened the thermos flask, pouring hot tea and they sipped from the same cup.

'How is it I tell you nothing and yet you know everything? The tea was warm and sweet and Ash's voice slurred as if intoxicated.

'Because,' her eyelids drooped, heavy with half sleep, 'you are the other half of me. You are everything that I am not, and all that I am. We see the world through different lenses, but in the end all our visions finish in the same place.'

At last Isabella stretched and rolled over, the curves of her breasts and hips accentuated by the turn. Like the Hindu goddess Parvati, she reached and began to pick the late blackberries from the brambles at her side. Her wrists and hands turned in a series of elegant mudra hand gestures, unharmed in the tiny gaps amongst the thorns. The fruit was swollen and too ripe. It stained her mouth and, he suspected, his as well, as she fed him like a mother bird. Squashing a fat overripe berry between his hands, he ceremoniously marked the centre of her forehead with purple juice, and she marked his. A jealous robin hopped up to join the feast, pecking the rejected berries at their feet, stopping every now and then to survey them with a watchful eye.

CHAPTER TWENTY-FIVE

On their way home storm clouds came in quickly. Ash and Isa ran the last leg up the hill but arrived soaked at the farmhouse. In the narrow hall, they wrestled muddy boots and dripping layers of clothing, laughing, trying to help each other. Ash hauling at Isa's right leg caused her to tumble gently backwards in the hall, her legs waving in the air. He pulled again at the heels until her boots slipped off but then he crashed back against the door frame. Crawling forward, she untied his laces and returned the favour. With muddy hands, he helped her up. Her face was red with wind and rain and there was a drip on the end of her nose. He offered her the sleeve of his sweatshirt to wipe it. Cheekily, she snuggled into his chest to stem any further flow. She smelt of sweet wet hay and stable, carrying a memory of the smoke from dung fires in Delhi in the winter when he was child.

In the kitchen, they peeled off jumpers, t-shirts, trousers, vests, and, like naughty children in shabby underwear, warmed themselves against each other and the Aga, kissing and swapping sides so each could warm their back in turn. Isa brought a tartan blanket and they wrapped themselves together in it, Ash leading Isa up the stairs.

The bathroom was all of her, of Yardley, of England. Like his bedroom it faced the back of the house. On one wall were two basins with a large mirror above them. Opposite them was a window with green and white peacock tail patterned curtains and a pot pourri on the sill. On the far wall there was a deep bath tub. Divesting herself of the blanket Isabella took a towel from the free standing pine rail and wrapped herself in it. Looking back at him, she crossed the room and began to run the bath. The plumbing drummed and whistled into tune followed by a pause before hot water poured from huge brass taps. He drew the curtains, unnecessarily, he knew for there was no one to see but the mountains, cows and sheep. He noticed that there were peacocks, some with tails spread, some in pairs inserted randomly as patterned tiles around the room. It might seem strange that she had chosen this motif, but he knew the answer without asking.

She came to him out of the mists of steam, helping him with his vest and his pants. It was business like, practical and neither was shy. It occurred to him that he had been cared for like this once before. He remembered the day his nanny, Pooja, had just disappeared. He had looked for her for days, in the bedrooms, in the kitchen, in the streets, shouting, crying and calling her name, reduced to hoping and waiting. Eventually his father told him that he was a man now and no longer needed a nanny and that Pooja had gone back to her village in Gujarat. Men don't cry. But it was as if his own mother had died. But now he was here in this peacock water garden with this alabaster goddess.

Shy now, she hid behind him, shampooing his hair with lavender bubbles. He inhaled, willing the fragrance to the depths of his lungs. Diving back with gentle waves, he rested his head, worshipping from below. She stroked the lather away, saving a little at the end to paint a moustache under his nose, curling the ends in handlebars high onto his cheeks. Scooping up a handful of foam, he spotted her breast with droplets of pearls and daubed her face with a beard of snow. Coaxingly gently, he brought her about, piling her hair on the top of her head, kissing her neck and lathering her in turn. Supporting her, she slipped between his legs and he pushed foam icebergs up against her thigh, watching as she emerged, golden hair swapped for brown.

'How did that happen?' he asked, puzzled.

She lay back on him.

'What?'

'The water it changes the colour of your hair when wet. '

'I don't understand.'

'My hair is always black; black when it is dry and black when it is wet, except these days with a little grey.' He was vaguely conscious that he had reverted to his old way of talking, the Americanisms gone. 'But your hair changes colour.'

She smiled, leaning back on him and running in more hot water from the tap with the aid of her toe. Closing his eyes, he accepted her weight letting it and the warmth of the water sooth the exertions of the day. He felt her raise herself and opening his eyes, watched as she emerged from the water, stepping from the bath.

'My God, You are so beautiful.' She dried her breasts and her thighs, unwinding like a cat, down her legs to her toes. Wrapping her hair in a smaller towel, she opened her arms, offering him another towel. He shook himself.

'Come here, shaggy dog!' She looked at him full on, enfolding him, pulling his head to her chest to dry his hair, patting his arm pits, his chest and kneeling to take his feet in her lap, wrapping them, him in softness.

She gave as she took, tuning herself to him and he to her, plucking the strings and sounding the drums, waiting, responding, with silent sound. He had never known such sympathy and it brought from some hinterland a rage of strength which many have tried to name. He did not know if it lasted a second, a year, or a mere breath, except that he had lived a lifetime within. He felt her give way and tried to catch her as she fell, but was already lost. She lay like a broken doll, beneath him, her neck twisted back to the left, her eyes rolled up in their sockets, her face bloodless white.

'Oh my love, my love. I should never have come. Forgive me!'

She was too heavy, almost, to pick up, as if all the weight in him had disappeared into her. He struggled to lift her, her head lolling back, cradling her to him and pressing his cheek to hers. She moaned quietly, curling tight to protect herself, as a baby in his arms. He held her, nursing with his hand, his mouth the tremors and aftershocks, rocking, cradling her to stillness.

CHAPTER TWENTY SIX

They awoke late to find a glorious sunny Sunday, the stream gurgling below the open fly window. In the kitchen they cooked breakfast together, bacon, scrambled eggs, tomatoes, and at Ash's insistence, baked beans on hot buttered toast. How he relished the slimy orange beans, smacking his lips with delight and how they both laughed! Then they were quiet again, looking at each other with a new intimacy, shy, afraid, both of them wondering how to live a life in a weekend. Both of them were aware that Ash would be leaving on Monday morning.

'I want to take you somewhere, show you something,' Isa said when they had finished stacking the dishwasher. 'The head of the Dale, the top of Top Hill, my favourite place in all the world.'

Taking the old Land Rover they set out up the Dale, the only road following the line of the river below. They passed two villages, a few scattered farms, the road narrowing to a single track, over a little stone bridge, higher they went, past the tree line. They stopped twice and Ash jumped out to open and close the gates. It was not long before they had left civilization behind. Without a word Isa stopped the car and they got out. They were in a beautiful desolate place, a world without gates and walls, high on the moor. The wind caressed their faces and tugged affectionately at their hair.

'Come,' Isa said shouldering the rucksack and taking his hand, her words disappearing on the air.

The day was moving faster now, the wind running in front of them, as wild hares through the grass and heather, green chasing purple, speeding, inking grey to blue at the top of Top Hill.

'When my boys were little, they used to call it the mountain that anchors the world to heaven.' Isabella raised an arm to point, her coat sleeve caught as a sail in the wind, her hair blowing and hiding her face. After about a hundred yards, the metalled road gave way to a grass lane but this soon petered out to narrow tracks which lost themselves in the heather. There was no obvious way but Isabella knew where she was going. They walked on for about an hour climbing gently all the while.

'Look!' she pointed again, 'ancient burial mounds.'

Ash was amazed to see three small green mounds in a dip in the land.

'People lived up here?'

She nodded. 'Thousands of years ago, perhaps lower down in the Dale, there we can still see the ancient field lines. These are probably tombs. Come and see!'

She led him to the front of the mounds and knelt down in front of them by some flat rocks.

'Cup and ring marks.' Ash saw the stones had been carved with very simple markings, a circle with a dot in the middle. Kneeling too, he traced them very lightly with his index finger, the circle and the dot, the circle and the dot.'

'What do they mean?' he asked.

Isa, shook her head. 'No one knows.'

They sat for a while in the shelter of one of the mounds watching the wind chasing the sunshine through the clouds. He felt himself unravelling like a coil inside, no longer sure what was real or not, what was up and what was down. In Dubai his world was straight lines, spreadsheets, graphs, angles, goals, targets, tall buildings, roads. Here with Isabella in this place, nothing was linear, everything was soft, yielding, contour and curve. It disorientated him.

'I think,' he said, at last, 'in life there are no lines, only circles.'

After a while they set out again, climbing steeply now up the side of the mountain, higher and higher, dragging, pulling each other, panting. He gripped hard with his hand to pull her up. The heather had passed away and there was only grass and rocks. The wind beat them, whipping their faces, robbing their words, so that they gave up trying to speak. On their hands and knees they scrabbled. Her nails scratched his forearm as he hauled her almost to the top. They were the world and the world was rock and stone and it was them. They climbed with a passion as if they were making the world anew. There were no boundaries. They ran, arms out stretched, through the bog cotton to the summit with the stone cairn, climbing to the very top, where the wind magically just died.

Exhausted, they nestled in the lea by the cairn. She did not attempt to name the dales, mountains, and villages that rolled out under seas of sky. As they watched, clouds floated in over Rolly Crags on the far side of the valley. One or two, then a few more, they played shadow football with the sunshine on the purple moor. All colours came, in a rush, red, green, yellow, blue, brown, indigo, orange and everything in between, melded into autumn gold, joining together at that moment in one place, and Ash knew a world that never was, but might have been.

'Come with me,' he said, 'back to Dubai.'

CHAPTER TWENTY SEVEN

Later that night, they lay naked together in the big bed in the stables, Isabella's head resting in the crook of Ash's shoulder. Gently, he stroked her tousled hair, fine, soft as silk, like that of a young child. It smelt of fresh Dales' air, of rain and sweat and wood smoke, all at the same time, causing him to marvel at how that could be. They had had a perfect last evening together. After a day walking, they were hungry and tired so Isabella had bought take away fish and chips from the pub. They had eaten them out of the paper with their fingers, sitting cross-legged in front of the fire at the cottage. Isa's face had been flushed from the sun, wind and rain. She wore no make-up. She was just herself. She had not given him an answer to his question and when he had pushed a little, she had looked lovingly into his eyes then tweaked his nose and traded a chip for a kiss. He could not begin to articulate his feelings, the blessing of finding her after so long, the agony of desire, the waiting, the tender yearning, the possession, the ecstasy and the deep, satisfying sleep that followed. After years of running from himself and the guilt of living a charmed life in his dead friend's shoes, he had found an inner stillness. Could he ever go back to the man he had been before meeting Isa again? He knew his answer. Had she not just given it to him here in the bed? She would return with him and the future was theirs to make together. He felt as if God, for His own reasons, had given both of them a second chance. He would give up the Dubai penthouse and buy some land where they could plan and build their home. It would be built just the way she wanted, with floor to ceiling folding windows and a view looking over the Arabian Sea. They would employ an architect and he would supervise the building himself. The house would not need to be large or ostentatious, just simple, minimalist in design with sufficient rooms to accommodate the boys when they came to stay. It would have a pool and a garden and in the winter months they would invite friends to candlelit dinners on the patio. Already, he saw Isabella, wearing white linen shorts and a pink T-shirt, working barefoot at a gigantic canvas in her new studio. He had come home early and she was quite unaware that he was standing motionless at the door, admiring her, loving her. He could see her brow furrowed in concentration and noticed that there were smudges of glistening orange and green paint on her nose so that she looked like a cheeky circus clown.

When the boys came, he would do his best to be an understanding and supportive stepfather. Although he knew that would be neither straightforward nor easy, he felt confident that he had much to offer them. On boat trips, the boys would laugh, the wind in their red hair. They would do a spot of fishing and barbecue their catch on the beach. Perhaps one of the boys might fancy a career in business or finance. If so, he was well placed to give them a head start.

Isabella's palm rested on Ash's chest. She felt his warmth against her bare breast and thigh and heard the beating of his heart, steady and reassuring with the regularity of a grandfather clock. She sensed his breathing slow and his muscles relax as he slowly drifted into sleep. She wanted the moment to last for ever. But it was not to be. Warm though she was, she began to shiver, an inner shaking deep inside her, as doubts, anxieties and fears crowded in on her: she had been here before, twenty-five earlier, only for the bliss of that time to be shattered. She remembered how uncertain, even reluctant, she had been to go to the reunion fearing that Ash might be there. How had she come to share her bed with him after all that had happened? Why had she let herself be drawn once more into the feelings that all those years ago had eventually driven her young self almost over the edge?

And now there was Tony and the boys. Already she was betraying them. That came at a price. She had broken her marriage vows and she felt sick to the core at the thought of it. Although Isabella had long ago given up on religion, her mother, a Spanish Catholic of the old school, had made sure that the church had got to her at a young age. Bishop Benedict, aided and abetted by a succession of priests, had done his work well. A sense of shame, sin even, deeply embedded since childhood, now welled up inside her. She knew what she had promised Tony: keep you only unto him until death do you part. Lying there beside Ash, suddenly she was confronting things that she had long forgotten or perhaps merely suppressed. Try as she might, she could not forget her mother's warning about becoming a 'fallen woman', a description that only twenty-fours earlier she would have regarded with derision. In one of those absurd mental connections of a brain in torment, she imagined herself buried up to her neck in sand

and being stoned to death for adultery by a band of leering, bearded men, egged on by Tony who had thrown the first stone. 'Whore! Burn in hell for your sin!'

She screwed her eyes tight to banish the nightmare. But it had shocked her, made her question herself even more. How could it be that even after all these years, she still had not truly set aside what she considered to be the misogynistic and mediaeval poppycock of orthodox religion. She had friends who had taken lovers or become divorced. They were fine people, not to be categorised as somehow inadequate or 'fallen'. Had Tony always been faithful to her? He had been away from home so much. How could she know and would it matter, could it matter, now that she herself had been unfaithful? Would his sin, if there were one, exonerate her own?

Isa could not deny that she had given herself readily to Ash. What they had shared was precious, special, and something to be grateful for, even treasured. She had no doubt. And yet was this how all lovers felt or was it a simply a delusion born of a temporary and overwhelming joy? Isa did not know the answer.

But what she did know was that she had a life changing decision to make. Her heart pounded inside her chest. She was terrified. What she had feared had come to pass. She had let loose the two opposites within her. She had chosen to do it and now the rational, sensible and pragmatic were at war with the passionate, creative, primal free spirit within. She had fobbed Ash off that afternoon and evening when he had asked her to come with him. She was guilty of that for she did not want the joy of being with him to end. The combatants, the opportunities, fears and guilt raged in her mind. Would, could, should she go with Ash when he left? What would her life be like if she did, and would she able to live with herself? Try as she might, she could not shed the image of the two of them living happily together. Money would not be a problem and they could carve out a new private world. They would camp in the desert, snuggled together under a blanket next to a fire and abandoned to the silence and majesty of the stars. As an artist, she would revel in a myriad new colours and sensations, sounds and sights.

Yet could she simply set Tony and the children aside? Did she still love Tony? They had built a family and enjoyed years of stability. Some say that is happiness. But Tony was not Ash and did not, perhaps never could, stir the feelings she had for the man lying beside her. Like most married couples she and Tony had rubbed along with good times and bad, trials and tribulations. In Tony's frequent absence, her own days had revolved around lost socks, sewing on shirt buttons or name tags, school runs, sleepless nights coping with sick children, shopping for food and preparing meals for the children and herself, and seemingly endless laundry. Her memories of their holidays were of airport delays and times that were never as good as she had hoped although always to some degree enjoyable. She had realised early on in the marriage that theirs was not a romantic love but both had kept up their roles as wife, father and parents doing what was expected and required. Her life with Tony had long since settled into a predictable routine, mirroring the tatty old teddy bear that had remained for years on an old family rocking chair in the corner of the kitchen. Her life thus far simply could not be measured against the joy, elation, desire, passion and the finding of herself when she was with Ash.

She turned to look at Ash, sleeping contently next to her. She was certain he knew nothing of her torment as she agonised over what to do next. Yet, even as she searched, she knew that no answer was possible. Just where did right and wrong lie for her? As soon as she found the answer she was seeking, she found good reason to dismiss it. It must have been like this for those of her friends who had struggled to decide whether to leave husband and family for someone else. She had never quite been able to understand how a seemingly happily married woman could abandon husband and children. Now, perhaps, she was a little wiser.

Although Isa was desperately tired, sleep eluded her. She tossed and turned. Her head pounded, her mind a battlefield of clattering contradictions. She knew she had to find an answer or she would go mad. Quickly, but quietly, she got up from the bed and tiptoed to the door. Crossing the yard, she unlocked the door to the main house.

CHAPTER TWENTY EIGHT

On Monday morning Ash woke at first light to the sound of rain. The room was cold and he rolled over seeking Isa's warmth, but she was gone.

'Isa?' he called. No answer. Pulling on his pyjama bottoms and sweatshirt he went down into the yard. The clouds hung heavy, grim with drizzle. The main door to the house was unlocked and he let himself into the hall.

'Isabella? Isa?' Again no response. She wasn't in the kitchen either but there was a light coming from the studio. The door squeaked as he pushed it open.

He found her there, fast asleep lying on the chaise longue in her green painting overalls. She had left the big spot light on illuminating the easel with the painting in all its glory. He realised that she must have got up in the middle of the night to paint. The evidence of her frenetic labour was scattered in abandoned chaos; tubes of paint half squeezed, messy easels, brushes of various sizes, water, solvent, jars.

'Isa?' he called softly, kneeling down beside the sofa. She was curled up like a cat, paint all over her overalls, on her hands, on her face, in her hair. Slowly, she opened her eyes, stretching, uncoiling herself, standing up.

He put his arm around her bony shoulders. They were knotted tight with tension.

'Hey there,' he said pulling her closer, 'What's the matter? It's all right.' They stared in silence at the painting. Clearly she had been working through the night to finish the piece, drawing together the colours as they had experienced them together the previous day on Top Hill. It was if she had pushed everything to the very edge, perspective, light, form, colour, passion, a frenzy that was almost madness, held together at the last moment with threads of gold.

'It's beautiful,' he said at last, 'Beautiful.'

'Yes,' she whispered.' I have been carrying the weight of it in my head all these years, struggling to get it out. Now, at last it is done and I am done too.'

She looked grey, exhausted, her eyes shrunken with effort and lack of sleep. She was suddenly hunched and old.

'What do you mean?' Ash asked.

'I don't think I will ever paint again.'

'Of course you will. Don't be ridiculous!'

'No. It's over. I'm used up.'

'You're just tired. Take a break for a few weeks and the inspiration will come again.' Ash sniffed, kissing her on the top of her head as if she were a little girl.

'Does the painting have a name?'

She shook her head.

'Then you should call it *Shakti*, the power of all creation. It is all of you, body and soul, in this holy place.'

'No.' She shook her head. 'It is all of us.'

They prepared their breakfast together in the kitchen, the Aga still humming, the second hand on the wall clock ticking each clumsy second. They moved in slow motion, pouring milk, scraping butter onto the toast, peeling apples, each noting every tiny movement of the other as if this would rein back time. They sat side by side at the table eating without looking at each other.

'Come with me,' Ash said again then 'Marry me!'

He saw the surprise in her face, her eyebrows raised, her brow furrowed. Had he really just asked her to marry him? She stared at him. He was deadly serious and then he saw the pain. She tensed, twisted and contorted with distress. The colour drained from her face until she was white as sheet. Her hands shook.

'I don't think that would be a good idea.' She said at last, her voice distant and trembling. It was a while before she could go on. 'Last night I couldn't sleep. I cannot remember the last time I was so happy, here this weekend with you, but I have broken my marriage vows. That's why I came down to paint. It's the only way I know to sort things in my mind.' She sighed and took a deep breath. 'Ash, imagine me in Dubai!'

'You would love it.'

'No, I would be lost without the green, the fields, the animals, the birds, the trees, the seasons. And what would I do with myself all day? Paint my nails, whiten my teeth and go to the gym?'

'It doesn't have to be Dubai. We could be based in the city but there's a whole world out there to paint. We could go anywhere you wish; Australia, Canada, India. New Zealand is so beautiful, an artist's paradise.' Confused, he reached out to place his arm around her shoulders, stroking her cheek which was still streaked with gold and green paint. 'And I have money. More than enough. You would never be cold again, I promise.'

She raised her head, standing up abruptly, the chair scraping painfully on the quarry tiles.

'I can't leave the boys.' She spoke coldly, picking up the breakfast plates with trembling hands and taking them over to the sink. Carefully she collected the empty teacups, one by one. Ash sat alone at the kitchen table.

'They're getting bigger now jaan, the boys. In boarding school most of the time. Our home would be their home and there would always be the holidays. They'd love Dubai. It's a young person's paradise.'

'No.' She squared up to him, her face contorted with a tangled agony of emotions; passion, anger, love, compassion, frustration, despair.

'I understand. You're their mother. I'll wait. In a few years they'll be men, off to university.'

She shook her head, wringing her hands, eyes spitting fury and for an instant Ash thought that she might spring at him.

'I can't ask that of you Ash. Life does not stand still. Not for any of us. The past has no future. The price is too high.' Her words were harsh and clipped but her voice broke with emotion at the end.

'But I love you,' he said lamely.

'And I care for you too, very much. Yes, I do love you,' she whispered.

'Then why won't you come with me? You wanted to come with me before, why not his time?'

She wiped her hands on the dishcloth in an effort to control the shaking and took a deep breath.

'Remember that I told you about the college reunion a few weeks ago?'

Ash nodded.

'When Joanna invited me I wasn't at all sure that I wanted to go. The truth is I was scared, terrified that you might be there. I was in two minds about whether I wanted to see you again, resurrect my feelings and disturb my life. '

'Then why did you go? You joked on the phone that you hated reunions.'

'Because I felt I owed it to Joanna. Also because I decided that if you were there I needed to find some closure on our relationship. It's twenty-five years since you walked out on me for someone else, an ideal Indian girl whom you had never even met!' She raised her hand to stop him interrupting. 'Ash, I trusted you completely. I felt so betrayed. I still struggle to understand how you could do what you did to me. Even after all these years I still can't really get my head round it. We had made plans together. Not me, not you, but us. We were so close, like love birds. All the time we were together, did you know that your mother was working on an arranged marriage? '

'I knew it was on the cards.'

'Then why on earth didn't you discuss it properly with me instead of simply telling me when you had already made up your mind? You of all people! You who could be so critical of some aspects of Indian culture. Surely you could have talked about it and we could have worked things out. Or perhaps you were just toying with me all along? Just another western girl?'

'No, Isa. It was never that. I was never just playing with you. You know that in your heart.'

'Yes perhaps I do now, but I didn't then,' she whispered, blinking back the tears and forcing her face into a composed expression.

'Indian families, an arranged marriage, religion, caste, all our baggage,' he went on. 'It would have been a very difficult thing to discuss. Perhaps it was asking too much of you to know the struggle I had to go along with my parent's wishes.'

'Perhaps it was asking too much of *you* to know how I would feel if you did.'

She sniffed and threw the tea towel aside.

'I don't think you have any idea of how much you hurt me, what a devastating effect your apparently casual choice had on my judgement, my confidence and my self-esteem. It almost destroyed me, being discarded and tossed aside like that. I felt utterly worthless, crushed, like a worm or a beetle. I married a man that I probably would not have done if it had not been for you and I have had to live with that. It took me years and more than a painful struggle to come to terms with what you did to me.'

'I am sorry Isa, I wouldn't treat you like that again. I'm a different person now, older and wiser, I hope.'

'So am I, and I have everything to lose. I am not prepared to risk anything like that again.' She took a deep breath and exhaled slowly to release her tension.

Ash shifted in his chair and wiped his brow. He was genuinely shocked. She was right. In being a good Indian boy and acquiescing to his parents' wishes, he had given too little thought to the impact on her.

She came to sit down, this time in the chair on the opposite side of the table to him.

'But I am happy with you,' he spread out his palms offering his hands to her with the gesture. 'I am at peace.'

'And yet you ask me to turn my whole life upside down for you, to give up my home, this place that I love, the farming community of which I am part. You ask me to abandon my beloved sons. They'll soon be doing vital public examinations, making important decisions about their future. You ask me to leave my friends and risk my career. You ask me to give up all of this and follow you? What if I reverse the question, and you must not assume that I would wish you to do this. Could you give up your life in Dubai and come and live with me here in the Yorkshire Dales?

He paused, taken aback. He had not thought of that possibility.

'I don't honestly know,' he said eventually.

'Then let me try to answer it for you. You would not be happy here. Your world is centred in the Middle East. It's about business, finance and money, lots of money. My priorities are about capturing my imagination in paint, sharing my experiences with friends, family and clients and, yes, becoming emotionally and intellectually richer thereby. Your kinds of riches are not my kind.'

'That's hard to take.'

'I know but I think it's true. What do you think? Well, could you give up your life in Dubai for me?'

He was silent. She waited for him to shake his head. When at last he did so, heavily, sullenly, with regret, she turned away to stack the dishwasher. Ash felt as if he had had the stuffing knocked out of him. He did not have the energy to offer to help.

Bending down, she put in the dishwasher tablet and switched on the machine. The water began to trickle and gush as if to sooth them. Isa turned and looked Ash gently in the eye.

'A long time ago you had to choose between your family and me. An impossible decision perhaps for how can we ever chose between those we love? You did what your family wanted.

Now you ask me to make the same choice.' Her whole body trembled with the effort of her speech.

Ash, you know that I care very deeply about you. I can't explain it because I don't understand it myself. I cannot give you what you seek. Each of us must find our own way.'

Ash gritted his teeth to control a surge of fury. In his disappointment and frustration the urge to hit her, this woman he loved, was almost overwhelming. Instead he turned sharply on his heels and concentrated on putting one foot calmly in front of the other until he had crossed the yard and climbed the stairs to his room. Taking a deep breath, unclenching his fists, rolling his shoulders, he kept focused on each task. Packing: toothbrush, *Acqua di Parma* aftershave, shaver, phone, charger, pyjamas, underpants and shirts, folded carefully, into a laundry bag he had brought for the purpose. By the time he returned to the kitchen Isa had washed and changed and was in the process of shutting up the house; turning off the water, turning the gas down on the Aga, watering the pot plants.

'Do you want some tea for the journey?' she asked gently, proffering an empty thermos flask as a peace offering. Shaking his head he took her in his arms. They stood in the middle of the kitchen for a long time, breathing each other in, listening to the beating of their hearts.

'I'll send you the painting- Shakti,' she said weakly at last. 'It won't fit in the boot of the car. Alexis can arrange the shipping. He'll complain like the devil about it, but tough.'

'No!' Ash held her face in his hands, looking at her tired pale blue eyes. 'You must keep it, a memory of us, together this weekend.'

'Don't worry. I'll keep the print,' she pulled away, forcing a smile. 'The original will look so much better on the wall of a swish apartment in Dubai. All that glorious light!'

And then there was nothing more to say. He picked up his bag and she walked with him through the now heavy rain across the yard to his car.

'Good bye Isabella.' He wound down the window and turned the key in the ignition.

'Good bye Ash.'

'Don't wait! Go inside! You'll get soaked.' He reversed, wheels crunching on the gravel, and pulled slowly up the hill out of the yard. Just before the gate he looked back in the rear view mirror. She was still standing there drenched now by the downpour, waving. The car turned into the lane and when he looked again she was gone.

Ash set out up the Dale, following the route they had taken the previous day. The rain was coming down harder, the wind whipping it across the road in gusty, opaque sheets. The windscreen wipers battled against the torrent and the car splashed through the puddles. He drove through villages with pigeons puffed fat in the trees, past a tiny old lady in a blue anorak and red wellies, bent double against the wind, then by farmsteads with sheep looking mangy and forlorn in the fields. Up on the moor it began to hail, gently at first, then harder, faster din da din da din da, ta ta ta ta, ta ta ta ta. Ash stopped the car to open the gates. The wind lashed, the icy pellets cut hard at his cheeks, water soaking down his neck but he did not care. He wanted to be beaten, thrashed, whipped and he wanted more, wanted to freeze, wanted pain to dull the pain. At the top of the Dale he parked the car and sat shivering, numb with wet and cold, staring down through the mists. The storm raged, swirling wave on wave, angry, black, khaki and grey. The wind howled, the rain drummed on the roof, on the windscreen until it became one almighty roar. And when at last it was over, when the clouds had passed and the wind eased, Ash was overcome with a great weariness. Cradling his head in his hands, he rested it heavily on the steering wheel and for the first time since his mother had died and Shiv had been burnt alive, he wept.

CHAPTER TWENTY NINE

Oxford, December 2010

It was five nights before Christmas. The chimney wailed and howled as if an evil host were battling it out in some distant obscure other world. It was a terrifying sound, a frenzy of wolves, witches, wizards, ghosts and goblins and far below the flames were dying. A large log crackled, collapsing in on itself like a small volcano, sending a cascade of golden sparks into the living room. Lying at Peter's feet, Foxy briefly raised a startled head then settled down again to slumber. Sir Peter did not stir. He had fallen asleep in front of the fire, his book open on his lap. After a holiday in Dorset, he had been inspired to re-read Thomas Hardy and had dropped off after the ill-fated night time encounter in the fir plantation between the beautiful Bathsheba Everdene and the red uniformed and gold buttoned Sergeant Troy. Suddenly Foxy pricked up her ears, opened her big brown eyes wider this time then stood up, listening intently. She began to wag her tail, banging it vigorously on the floor to alert her master.

'What is it girl?' Sir Peter yawned and stretched. Foxy barked loudly. Despite her cuddly appearance the old mongrel was quite a fearsome guard dog. Picking up the poker from the hearth, Sir Peter kicked off his slippers and walked barefoot behind her into the kitchen. But then something extraordinary happened. Foxy stopped barking, listened and began whining and scratching at the back door as if something or someone were in pain.

Then it came, a gentle knock. If it had not been for Foxy Sir Peter would never have heard it.

'Who's there?' Sir Peter called, sounding more confident than he felt. It was a foul night and there had been a speculative burglary further down the street barely a fortnight before. There was a pause then an answer, a man's voice, soft and unsteady as if the speaker might have had a cold or sore throat.

'It's me, Sir, Misra. Ash Misra.' Sir Peter hurried with the two locks at the door and uncoupled the safety chain Irene had had installed after her mother's death. The visitor stared at the surprised octogenarian barefoot in his old red and blue striped pyjamas and tea-stained dressing gown.

Ash stood there under the halo of porch light, a wild man, eyes grey and unseeing as stone, yet agitated, darting here and there as if ready for a fight. Fists balled in his pockets, his face tense, cheeks sunken, pinched purple with cold, he was wound up like a boxer anticipating threats everywhere, ready to snap. Ill dressed for the weather, his brown suede brogues and the bottom of his chinos and black wool coat were caked in mud. His long grey beard and unkempt hair, glistened with a few flakes of snow making him old beyond his years. At the sight of the vagabond before him, Sir Peter hesitated. What had brought the once handsome young cricketer to this? But Foxy had no doubts or second thoughts. Tail wagging, whining softly she went to him and when the stranger offered her his chapped red hand, she licked it.

'Sir Peter? It's me, Misra, Ash Misra,' the vagabond repeated as if trying to convince himself, his breath short in his chest. 'I remember you were kind to me many years ago when I was a student and…' he stuttered with exhaustion, 'And you always told me to use the back door.'

'Well, come on in man, you look frozen, hurry up!'

Ash stood giant like, dripping wet, shivering in the tiny kitchen.

'I'm just tired. I just can't do it anymore,' he stuttered between chattering teeth. 'I'm sorry. I'm frightened. I didn't know where else to go.'

Dr Vic Samuels came the following day after morning surgery. He was an old school type nearing retirement and had supported Rosalind and Sir Peter through her illness to the end. So he bent practice rules and made a house call as a personal favour to Sir Peter. Dressed in his usual trade mark professional attire, a pink bow tie, white shirt, and morning suit trousers with matching waistcoat, he sat at the kitchen table slurping a mug of the old Master's best Co-op 99 builder's tea.

'It happens to the best of us,' Vic said dunking his ginger nut into his tea. 'The human brain is hard wired to rationalize. It wants order, to create sense, to put things right and will keep on computing until it has achieved this. The problem comes when, try as it might, it can't square the circle. In the end it overheats, short circuits, fizzy, bang, pop!' The old medic clapped his hands to illustrate his point. 'Sometimes the tiniest of matters can bring it on, the straw that breaks the camel's back.'

Sir Peter nodded and said, 'There is still so much of the world of the mind and spirit that we do not understand.'

Like the doctor, he was old and wise and too many times in

his life he had seen that look in a man's eyes when he had had enough, sometimes manic, sometimes lizard like, sealed over, scaled; during the war in the jungle, at the Japanese surrender, in interrogation rooms and police cells and in the offices of the privileged and powerful muffled by oak panels and leather chairs, behind closed doors. It was something that one never discussed. And once even on Foreign Service he himself had stared, teetered and fallen, briefly, almost, he knew, into the abyss.

'I've prescribed Mr Misra some anti-depressants. I don't think he is delusional in a serious way, more worn out, emotionally beyond exhaustion. They take several weeks to work properly but in the first instance they will help him sleep. He tells me he has been travelling and hasn't been sleeping for over a month now.'

Sir Peter offered Vic another ginger nut from the packet in the middle of the kitchen table. Both men took one and dunked in contemplative silence.

'Ash was in the UK in October to see an old friend,' Sir Peter broke in. 'After that he went to KL, Singapore, Hong Kong and then New York. He told me last night that at first everything was a little grey and then it got worse and worse. He came to London for a meeting this week and woke up in a hotel room having no idea where he was. He doesn't really remember how he got to Oxford or me.'

'Perhaps his subconscious was bringing him back to somewhere he remembered as safe? Anyway I don't want him travelling anywhere at present, certainly not internationally over the festive season. He tells me he has no family in the UK. I could admit him, but frankly, Peter, he would be better here initially at least, if you can cope? His perspectives should start to return once he has had a few decent night's sleep. I'll keep a close eye on him, pop in again in again in two days. In the meantime if there's anything, don't hesitate to ring me.'

Time passed slowly at first, Ash dozing most of the day in Rosalind's old rocker next to the fire, all the while Foxy refusing to leave his side. She would rest on his feet and stand sentinel at the bathroom door. She was even allowed to break house rules and sleep at the foot of the guest's bed at night. Ash was an easy visitor. He accepted the need for rest and treatment and ate whatever humble meal Sir Peter produced, though in truth, he had little appetite. He had more energy in the evenings and the first task he undertook was to bring in the wood and lay and light the fire. There was comfort in the routine and Ash would sit for hours watching the rise and fall of shapes and shadows in the flames, though he never told Sir Peter what he saw there and Sir Peter never asked.

On Christmas Day they were invited to lunch at the neighbours' next door. Sir Peter's son lived in America, and this year his daughter, Irene, and her family had decided to go skiing in Austria over the break which would have left him alone if fate had not brought Ash to his door. They went round at noon, bearing a Marks and Spencer's Christmas pudding, a tub of brandy sauce, a bottle of St. Emilion and a box of Thornton's chocolates. Cathy and Rick Wilson were both medics, he a consultant anaesthetist, she a GP. Cathy greeted them cheerfully at the front door with a sunny smile, bashfully hiding the dish cloth behind her back. She was accompanied by two bouncy children. Eva, aged nine, had tired eyes as if she had been up since the crack of dawn. Jack declared himself to be seven then surfed on a rug runner down to the end of the hall.

'Come and see my Star Wars Lego!'

They made up a small party that Christmas Day, just the six of them. The living room was strewn with presents; new red and blue jumpers, pyjamas, a pink elephant, an art kit, a chemistry kit, and two shiny new cricket bats: both children, boy and girl, were cricket crazy. The atmosphere might have been awkward but the children soon broke down all barriers and Rick was a stocky. easy going chap who gave the impression of having had a dose too many of his own anaesthetics. Before long he and Ash were sitting cross-legged on the floor building a Lego space ship. They all helped to carry dishes to the table and the children settled down, being polite, on their best behaviour as no doubt ordered to do.

'So you like cricket?' Ash asked Jack passing the Brussels sprouts to Rick and nodding to the cricket bats on the sofa.

The lad smiled from somewhere beneath his long blond fringe.

'I've got Michael Vaughan's autograph.'

'Wow!' Ash made his eyes wide with surprise.

'Me too!' the elder sister intervened assertively.

'That's fantastic! Perhaps you can show me after lunch. Would you believe me if I told you that I met Viv Richards at a party? Do you know who he is?'

'Of course we do! He was a West Indian cricketer. One of the greatest batsmen of all time!' Eva flicked her hair way that was so sophisticated and superior that Cathy burst out laughing.

'What Mum? Girls can play cricket just as well as boys!' Sniff, hand on hip. What attitude!

'Of course they can, darling! Now eat your carrots and sprouts.'

With that settled, things progressed to the pulling of crackers, the reading of jokes, and a grand flambé of the Christmas pudding which filled the room with a delicious brandy aroma.

Sir Peter saw that Ash, who had shaved for the occasion, was putting on a brave face, pushing through his exhaustion for a few hours at least. But the dimple cheeked, down to earth GP was not fooled. She saw the shadows round Ash's eyes and the effort in his face, yet she never asked, accepting his presence as he accepted her welcome. After the Queen's Speech, Jake and Eva were desperate to try out their new cricket bats so an impromptu game ensued in the back garden. The grey and blue wheelie bins were wickets, the batsman's end placed on the patio so the ball would bounce free of the muddy lawn. They formed two teams, boys against girls. Sir Peter, who under the influence of alcohol was feeling his age more than usual, acted as umpire. The children had their own well-established rules for garden cricket; four at the flower beds, sixes had to hit the fence. Anything that went into a neighbour's garden counted as a no ball. And so they played, somewhat ridiculously in the cold and the mud in an assortment of ill-fitting Wellington boots that Cathy had somehow collected and efficiently fitted to her guests. Sir Peter took his duties seriously and was scrupulously fair, allowing both children to have quite an innings. Eva was far better coordinated than her brother but he made up the deficit with chatter, vigour and enthusiasm which infected them all.

'Howzat! Six! Catch! Slog it! Run!'

Ash too played his part, dramatically leaping to catch one of

Eva's lofty sixes but deliberately dropping it at the last.

'Butter fingers!' Rick winked a conspiratorial thanks to Ash and he winked back. He later adopted the same strategy to give his son the same advantage. By the time light faded, they were all wet and covered in mud but there were smiles all round. Sir Peter, ever the diplomat, declared the match a draw.

'Rematch, rematch!' shouted Jack, pushing his fringe out of his eyes. Troubles were all forgotten for a while and though Sir Peter's hip ached, it did not feel like pain.

The New Year brought a tight lipped Irene and her journalist husband, Philip, for the day. Sir Peter took them all out for lunch at the *Trout Inn* and argued, affectionately, with Ash about who should pay. Ash was having none of it and won the day, having got on rather well with Philip and made an ally of him over a pint of beer during lunch.

After lunch they took a bracing short walk along the river path. On their return Philip and Ash lagged behind, deep in conversation. This gave Irene her chance with her father. 'But who is he? I mean what do we actually know about him? What does he want?'

'Don't worry! He's not after your inheritance if that's what you mean.' Sir Peter replied, quickening his pace so that Irene had to hurry to keep up with him.

'Don't be so naïve Dad,' she hissed. 'Think about it. It's odd, him living with you in this way. People will talk. He's after something. He must be.' Sir Peter pulled a bread roll out of his pocket that he had saved from lunch and stopped to feed the geese. He was not going to dignify any of it with a reply.

The days passed, and Ash became more himself, the tension easing visibly in him, his movements becoming more languid, his smile easier, more frequent. Every morning and afternoon, he would take Foxy on increasingly long walks in the Parks much to the animal's surprised delight. Once a week, he went to the surgery for a double appointment with the old doctor. Without doubt, the faithful, unquestioning old dog was the best nurse and the greatest part of the cure. In time Ash graduated to meeting once a fortnight and Sir Peter and Ash started cooking together, although Ash admitted at the outset that he was a lousy chef. Most of his life he had had staff to cook for him or he had bought take-aways or eaten out. Despite age and inexperience, neither man was willing to compromise. Ready-made sauces were not an option. Diligently, they sourced fresh spices from a shop in the Covered Market and were like young chemistry students, grating, chopping, pounding, grinding and critically sniffing the results of the blending in the mortar. Soon the kitchen was warm with mouth-watering scents; cumin, peppers, cinnamon, ginger, cardamom, chillies, garlic, onions in hot spluttering ghee. The aromas stirred up memories and emotions in Sir Peter's mind. The old India, British India, stories that people blocked their ears to, sanctimoniously censored, wrote off, deleted as politically incorrect, no longer wanting to hear. At first he hinted at things and was surprised when Ash was interested, asking searching questions, soliciting more. They conjured recipes from Ash's memory of his mother's home cooking and Sir Peter's recollections of food he had enjoyed himself as a young man in messes, restaurants and bazaars. He remembered a famous place in old Mughal place in old Delhi, by the Jama Masjid; fabulous mutton and roti. What was its name? Their increasingly ambitious cooking endeavours were supplemented by Internet searches and Cathy's tattered copy of Madhur Jaffrey's cookbook plus her own invaluable practical experience. There were a few disasters but on the whole they both got quite good at it and came up with the concept of Friday night as curry night. Cathy and Rick's nanny, grateful to be able to sign off early, would deliver the little darlings to the back door after school. Aprons in hand, they clamoured to make chapatis with Ash. He showed them how to roll the flour into round circles then pat them out with a little round ended wooden tool he had bought specially for use on the griddle. When they were cooked, Sir Peter would spread butter and marmite on them while they were hot, and they would all tuck in to the unorthodox but delicious snack. It kept them going until their parents returned around six.

And so it was over the cooking and the chores that Ash and Sir Peter talked. Sometimes it was over the soap suds, the pink plastic washing up bowl, while hanging out the washing on the line, or feeding the birds with stale chapatis, or while wheeling a squeaky trolley around *Tesco's*. Ash confessed that he had once accidentally burnt quite a large hole in the carpet in his College room with a cigarette. So terrified had he been that he might be sent down for the offence, that he had rearranged all the furniture in his room and not told the scout. Sir Peter responded by admitting that he feared he had left a lengthy unpaid bar tab at the Bombay Gymkhana club at Christmas in 1946.

'No worries! Ash quipped. 'I'll settle it for you next time I'm in town!' To this Sir Peter responded that in that case he would be happy to write off the carpet damage. And from such banter other conversations began to flow, Ash talking about his family's horrendous flight from Lahore to Delhi in August 1947, how his maternal grandfather had been a broken man after partition. On his death bed he thought he was back in his bedroom in the old family house in Lahore overlooking the rose garden, and had kept blathering on about the scent of the sweet peas and asking Ash to nip down to Fazal's Sweets by the Mochi Gate and bring him back some of his favourite mithai.

Ash sighed at this recollection. 'Perhaps that is why my generation of educated Indians have been so keen to jump ship and move abroad. Our ancestral homes, our lands were lost. Can you blame us? We're the children of refugees with shallow roots.'

Days passed quickly with easy routines, turning into weeks then months and they were happy for a while a least, this unlikely duo. Ash bought a laptop and began writing a business plan. His spreadsheets grew with every passing day, but he always had time to play knock-about cricket with Rick and the children in the cold. By the beginning of February Ash's Blackberry began to bleep and Sir Peter heard the eager buzz in his voice and saw the twinkle in his eyes at a renewed sense of purpose. It pleased him that Ash was well again, but at the same time he was sad, for he knew it would soon be time for the younger man to leave.

When spring came, they celebrated Holi with Cathy, Rick and the children, Ash having miraculously obtained coloured powder paint via an Indian restaurant on the Cowley Road. They had one crazy, mad, wild, spring fiesta in Sir Peter's garden, screaming, shouting, whooping, chasing, trying to cover each other with as much paint as possible, raising clouds of red, yellow and purple into the air. When the children and their mother ambushed Ash, Rick and Sir Peter behind the apple tree, the young ones jigged with delight. Not to be outdone, the men trapped them behind the garden table to take revenge. In the end when all the ammunition was finally used up and the lawn, trees, flower tubs, sundial, climbing frame and wheelie bins were daubed, spotted and streaked with colour, they all flopped, panting, into garden chairs. They resembled a ridiculous assortment of large fluorescent marker pens. Sir Peter looked at Ash, his paint daubed face creased with laughter, and saw that the younger man was himself again.

CHAPTER 30

Birmingham, Winter 2011

Ferdie ambushed his mother at the kitchen sink. Encircling her in his long arms, he bent to bury his head in her neck. He smelled of deodorant and hair gel and Isabelle loved him for it.

'You alright, Mum?'

'Fine,' she replied brightly. But she knew he was not convinced and his unexpected affection almost breached her defences. She desperately needed someone in which to confide. She was tempted, so tempted to tell him about Ash and how since they had parted it was as if she had lost her muse. A painting commission of Upper Wharfdale in spring was overdue but when she stood at the easel she saw only a fog of black and white. But how could she tell her son that she and his father had not been intimate for over five years and that it hadn't been for want of encouragement on her part. She had had celibacy imposed upon her. No. She couldn't tell him that. It wouldn't have been fair to burden the boy. She blinked back the tears. Dear Ferdie, he had always been able to read her emotions, seen through her forced jollity and repertoire of carefully orchestrated fun outings and little treats. It was a damp Sunday afternoon in mid-February and Isabella had been washing up after tea. They had spent a rare weekend with them all at home at the same time; the boys on exeat and Tony back from business travels. On the Saturday evening they had all snuggled up on the sofas to watch a film, and taken a brisk, muddy walk together in the park on the Sunday morning. Both activities had required Isabella to issue a three line whip. For lunch she had cooked a good old fashioned Sunday roast beef and Yorkshire puddings, finished with plum crumble and vanilla ice cream. It was everyone's favourite. Afterwards, Tony had stacked the dishwasher, refused a cup of tea and left for London around 3pm. A junction was closed on the motorway so he had left early to make part of the journey before the daylight went completely. All in all the weekend hadn't gone too badly, Isabella thought with relief. Timely interventions on her part had defused any potentially blazing rows. But she could no longer convince herself all was well. Composing her face, she turned to her son and tidied his fringe with her hand. It was a ruse to smooth out the furrows of concern from his brows.

'Love you, Mum.' He kissed her on the top of the head.

'Love you too.'

Ferdie turned away to pack his holdall which lay in the corner of the kitchen. In another half an hour Isabella would drive the twins to the station to catch the train back to school. He dithered then came back to his mother, taking his hands in hers.

'Mum, Jamie and I were talking about it on the train on the way home on Friday.'

'Talking about what?'

'About you Mum.' The young man took a deep breath. 'We know you've stayed with Dad for us.'

The breath stopped in Isabella's chest.

'But we're big now, sixteen next month.' Ferdie continued, emboldened since he had had the courage to broach the subject. 'It's such hard work for us all when Dad is around. To be honest, it would be easier without him and you are so much more relaxed when he's away. He's hardly here anyway, never has been. Ever since I can remember he's been coming and going. You've brought us up virtually on your own.'

Isabella felt as if the ground were shaking under her feet, the room jumping and shuddering around her. The boy's words triggered an earthquake in her mind. It came to her as a vision of the beautiful façade of a typical Andalusian Church, it was her ideal of family, duty and doing the right thing. Helpless, she watched as it crumbled to dust. Registering the shock and distress in his mother's face, Ferdie squeezed her hands.

'Mum, you've done so well in your career and everything. Jamie and I are so proud of you. But soon enough we'll be off leading our own lives.' He put his right arm around her shoulders and danced his left hand in the direction of the kitchen door. 'I'm just saying, you don't have to stay with Dad for us, not if he makes you so unhappy. You're still young. You've got your own life to live.'

By the time Isabella returned from the station it was a bitterly cold night. She wheeled the bins out for the morning collection, the frost on the pathway glistening like diamond dust in the moonlight. Back in the house she folded some sheets and towels. Usually doing the laundry was calming; the smell of warm cotton, smoothing out the creases with the flat of her hand. But routine domestic therapy did not work that evening. Her mind was spinning. About a week after she and Ash had parted, she had sent him a *Whats App* message asking for his postal address in Dubai so she could arrange the shipping of *Shakti*. There had been no reply. Christmas had come and gone and Isabella had chided herself. What did she expect? She had rejected Ash and he had moved on. Then late last Wednesday she had received a text message from an unknown UK mobile number.

Hello from Oxford!
  Sorry for not replying sooner. I have been unwell. Am better now. Don't worry. Starting new job in London in March. Currently looking for accommodations. Will let you new address asap.
  Love, Ash

Isabella had not replied. She did not know what to say. Closing the door to the airing cupboard, she gave a heavy sigh and rolled her shoulders. She felt battered and bruised, every bit of her aching with fatigue. Going back downstairs, she curled up on the sofa to watch an old episode of *Yes Minister*. Usually that cheered her up. Eventually she made herself a cocoa, had a hot bath then went to bed. She slept fitfully. She was in her nightdress and wellies, lost on Droverdale Moor, snow swirling around her. In the distance she could see the lights of the village but the mist was scudding down from the hills. She tried to outrun it but the snow was too deep. She fell, she called for help but the silence swallowed her cries. She was so cold, so very cold, then blackness.

Isabella woke just after six am. Her head and neck ached. Barefoot, she went down to the kitchen, her knees clicking on the stairs. There was no Aga in the Birmingham house and the central heating had not yet come on. Shivering, she pulled her old pink dressing gown tight around herself. Without thinking, she boiled the electric kettle, made a cup of tea and sat the kitchen table in the yellow light of a nearby street light. She put on the radio and lazily flicked through a collection of photographs on her iPad that she had taken last year of Upper Wharfdale in spring. How to inspire her mind for a day's creative work? Never before had she failed to deliver a commission on time. Rain tapped insistently on the window and she felt herself drifting toward the steely black rocks that constituted the reef of failure in her mind.

Suddenly, the news reader's voice, cut through her melancholy.

'The on-running expenses scandal has claimed its latest victim. Last night Joanna Althrope MP announced she would be standing down at the next general election. This follows an enquiry into her expenses claims by the House of Commons Standards and Privileges Committee.'

CHAPTER THIRTY ONE

Oxfordshire Winter 2011

It was getting on for nine-thirty am when Isabella arrived at Joanna and Gus's house. She was greeted by two police officers and a shabby press pack who were leaning on their vans sipping cups of tea from thermos flasks. She rang the buzzer at the gates. As they opened the reporters skipped half-heartedly forward in the hope of a glimpse of the designated villain of the day; Joanna Harrington. Gus had walked up from the house with the dog to greet Isabella and waited on the other side of the gates. He put the animal on the back seat of her car and got in beside her for the drive to the house.

'Going to be a lovely day,' he said.

Isabella nodded. She had left the rain behind in Birmingham and the skies were a startling winter turquoise.

'How is she?'

Gus shrugged.

'You know Joanna. She's a fighter. Thanks for coming. We're *persona non grata* in certain circles at the moment. It's at times like this when one discovers who one's true friends really are.' He didn't give Isabella time to respond. Now he had started talking he wanted to get everything off his chest.

'She's not guilty you know. She's not a criminal, not a fraud-ster. The whole thing's a farce, and the tragedy is that she's a damn good MP. She's worked her socks off for this constituency and everything she claimed for was approved. Gus grimaced. 'And I guarantee that we don't own a duck house, nor do we have a wisteria, and I have never used a trouser press in my life! He gestured with an air of despair to the view over the estate, a lattice work of naked tree branches black against the sparkling sky. 'I blame it all the on the bloody bankers. Some MPs tried to keep up with them, flipping this and that, allowances, not expenses, and then the press moved the goal posts and they were all caught offside. Sycophantic bunch bankers, free riding on other people's innovation and ideas! You wouldn't believe the kind of stories Joanna was getting from local businesses in her surgery after the financial crisis. Small businesses being sold interest rate hedging products they didn't understand when all they wanted was a small business development loan. If things had been like that in my day, my business would never have got off the ground. Scandalous!'

All was quiet at the house. They entered via the back door to the servant quarters, past the dog basket, piles of wellies, and mounds of Barbours, fleeces and flak jackets hanging on the wall.

'I managed to persuade Joanna to stay away from the House of Commons today and she's decided to tidy the bloody kitchen instead.' Gus whispered conspiratorially to Isabella.

'Look who's here to see you darling,' he announced, opening the door.

They were greeted by Joanna's large backside squeezed into a pair of black jeans. She was down on her hands and knees surrounded by piles of pots, pans, baking tins, cake moulds and assorted kitchen paraphernalia. The kitchen table was laden with bunches of flowers. She spun around and sat up on her haunches, her hands resting on her plump thighs. Unmade up she wore a baggy grey sweat shirt, but her hair had recently been cut and coloured and the style was holding up well.

'Ever wondered what the end of a political career looks like?' Joanna quipped, lifting her head and spreading her arms out wide to indicate the chaos around her. And then she roared with laughter.

'Having a bit of a clear out?' Isabella rolled up her sleeves. 'Need some help?'

Gus reached out a hand and hauled his wife to her feet and the two women embraced.

'I'll put the kettle on,' Gus said. 'Then I'll leave you girls to it.'

'All the best political campaigns finish in someone's kitchen with a bottle or two or three and a brew. Cheers!' Joanna said. The two women sat at the table dunking Hobnobs into large mugs of coffee. 'Isa, you look awful.'

'So do you,' Isa responded. 'I'm so sorry, Jo.'

Joanna shrugged.

'Don't be. Politics is a mug's game and I've had a good innings. But hell, I'll miss it. I loved being an MP, being in the thick of things, the hustle and bustle, the drama, the ringing of the division bells on the night of a big vote. I joined the Party to help people and I've done my best and been true to my principles. I know that even if others don't. I have had so many emails of support and just look at all the flowers!'

Isabella smiled.

'You worked hard for people in the constituency and they know it.' She paused to arrange a bunch of carnations that had been haphazardly stuck into a vase.

'So what next?'

'Retire and write my memoir. *She's a Bolshy Bird, My Career in Parliament* or some such nonsense!' They laughed at the ludicrousness of the notion that Joanna could ever take it easy.

They finished their coffee and set to wiping down the lower kitchen cupboards, clattering and banging about, vigorously ordering the kitchen utensils. Joanna looked at her friend out of the corner of her eye and waited. A life time in politics had given her a sixth sense.

Isabella tidied the nest of three cake tins, placing one inside the other.

'I've decided to leave Tony.' The words had slipped out of Isabella's mouth before she knew it.

'Bravo! About bloody time!' Joanna beamed and clapped her hands.

'Best news I've heard in ages. That man's been keeping you on a leash for years.'

'I wouldn't say that. He just doesn't have any imagination. That's the problem and I can't pretend anymore. I'm tired of being the one who takes all the initiatives.'

Joanna nodded politely.

'When did you decide?'

'Last night. Actually, I've had a little affair.' Isabella blushed. She couldn't believe she was telling Joanna this. 'I am not leaving Tony for him, for the other man. It's just the look of joy on someone's face when they are pleased to see you, when they cradle your face in their hands, like this.' Tenderly, Isabella touched her friend's puffy red cheeks. 'The affair, it made me realise what was possible in life.'

'Fantastic! This calls for champagne.' Joanna stood up and triumphantly pulled a bottle out of the fridge.

'Always keep one on ice. Never know when it might be needed!' The two women sat cross-legged on the kitchen floor, drinking bubbly out of crystal glasses. They laughed until they cried.

'Here's to us!'

CHAPTER THIRTY TWO

Isabella never intended to go into Oxford that afternoon. After a light lunch with Joanna and Gus, she took a siesta on a bed in a guest room. Before she knew it she was on the A34 driving into town. There had been a lot of rain and the sunshine glistened on the mini lakes in the flooded fields creating a foreign land. She felt strangely elated, giddy almost. Stopping in the car in the Park and Ride, she pulled out her phone and wrote a text message

'Hi Ash. Am in Oxford this afternoon. Are you still here? Isa?' Send.

Almost instantly she saw that he was typing a reply. She hadn't expected that, not really. *'Yes. Lodge. College 3.30pm?'*

'OK. CU there.'

Isabella got off the bus in the centre of Oxford, crossed the road and turned into Broad Street. She had walked this route to College a thousand times. Her feet needed no direction. They knew where to go. She ran her hand along the wall where she used to secure her bike. She was calm, no longer anxious or afraid. She was going home.

She stepped over the high wooden threshold through the little wooden door into College. There he was, standing there in a black wool coat, red scarf and blue beanie hat, waiting for her in the exact spot where they used to meet to go out all those years ago. She had not known what to expect and was prepared for anger or hostility. That would have been natural after Droverdale. But when it came to it, it was the easiest thing in the world. He just opened his arms to her and gave her a big hug.

The Tack Room was warm and smelt of coffee and freshly baked cakes. Isabella and Ash sat upstairs on opposite sides of the distressed oak table overlooking the street. In the no man's land between them lay a red teapot, two spotted mugs, a jug of milk, two plates and forks and a large piece of carrot cake. Ash cut this in two, kept one half for himself and put the other on a plate for Isabella He pushed this to her side of the table. They had arrived at a quiet time and were the only customers but still spoke quietly to avoid being overheard.

'Sir Peter introduced me to this place.' Ash tore the top of a sachet of sugar and tipped in into his tea. 'I've been staying with him since Christmas. He's been amazing, like a father to me.'

'I am sorry to hear you have been unwell. What was the matter?' Isa asked gently. 'You look good actually. Better than you did in Droverdale, younger, more relaxed.'

'I've had some kind of nervous breakdown, a mini depression.'

'Oh God, Ash. You should have said. You should have called. I'm so sorry if I caused something like that.'

'No, Isa, heaven forbid. It's complicated, been a long time coming. I can see that now. In a way it's a good thing. It's forced me to stop, given me time to think and reassess my priorities.' He took a mouthful of carrot cake. 'Yum! This is good. To be honest, I'm pleased you texted me today. I've been wanting to talk to you. I've never really tried to explain why I made the decision I did, the…' He stopped as if choking on the rest of the sentence.

'Ash, it doesn't matter anymore. It was all so long ago. And I too have got something to tell you.'

He laughed.

'Confession time, then ladies first! I insist.'

Isabella took a deep breath.

'I've decided to leave Tony.' She raised her hand to pre-empt his intervention. 'It's long overdue. I should have done it years ago.'

Ash pushed back his wispy, greying fringe.

'Pffff! That's a surprise. And what about the boys?'

'They're cool about it. In the end, it was they who made me realise that things couldn't carry on the way they were. It was making them miserable too. Both Tony and I are at fault. We've never faced up to reality and we let things fester. A divorce, a clean break will be better all round.' She lowered her eyes to the blue, yellow and green spots on her teacup.

'It's funny,' she continued. 'Now the decision is made I feel light headed, high almost. It's as if I have been living life with a millstone around my neck.' She smiled and cocked her head to one side. 'Now it's your turn. Tell me about the job?'

'The job is the easy part. A friend of mine, a retired Swedish banker, has set up a new venture to collaborate with and invest in start-ups. It has a focus on sustainable technology and concepts that break the mould. We've raised a good chunk of capital and put in some of our own money. I'll be working out of London with young entrepreneurs in Europe and the Middle East. I'm excited about it. It's something new and worthwhile.'

'Sounds good,' Isabella noted the sparkle in his eyes and

pronged a piece of carrot cake.

Ash sighed and looked out of the window watching a young Chinese man in ridiculously tight drainpipe jeans and red trainers push his bicycle up the cobbled street.

'I don't know what I was expecting when I got the India scholarship and arrived in Oxford. In some ways I was disappointed. The British India looted India, right? I had imagined that the streets would be paved with gold. Parts of London were so shabby and I was shocked when I saw poor white people doing manual work. I'd never imagined that. But there I was, the son of refugees with a prestigious scholarship at one of the best universities in the world. I wanted to understand how it was that the people of this tiny, rainy, boggy, barbarian island had managed to build such a massive Empire. I wanted to succeed. I needed to succeed.

'We all did. 1980s Oxford was mad. It was as if there were a 'make money' virus in the air. Like it or not, it infected us all.'

Isabella nodded.

'You could taste it, smell it and when we graduated we were like greyhounds out of the traps. There was a real sense the world was on the cusp of change. Deng Xiao-ping's' reform and the opening up in China and later Manmohan Singh in India. I don't think people in the west comprehend the scale of what had happened in these two countries.' He sighed and his face clouded over. 'Looking back, the Delhi I grew up in was a closed world. My father was so proud of his subscription to *Time Magazine*. It came by airmail every week. He thought it made him international! And can you believe it? There was only one international news programme on the TV per week. At university the whole college crowded into the Common

Room to watch it. We young ones, we were thirsty. We were hungry. We wanted more than the Congress led socialist style command economy. It was killing us, stifling us. I remember the feeling, it was like death by a thousand cuts. At that time our career paths were constrained; civil service, army, air force, medicine, engineering or law. It was what we were bred for, what everyone expected of us.' Ash put his hands on his head. 'Our Delhi world, it was stale, stagnant, government controlled. There was no such thing as imagination, entrepreneurship or self-fulfilment.' He took a large slurp of tea and offered his cake to Isabella. She shook her head.

'Don't say I don't love you,' he joked. 'I have just offered you my last piece of cake.'

She reached out and briefly stroked his hand.

'My large extended family was such a crowd. Two sets of grandparents, a host of aunts and uncles, all refugees from Lahore, all deeply scarred by the horrors of Partition. But I would be lying if I said that the family wasn't nurturing when I was small. There was always an aunty to blow my nose or paint antiseptic on a cut knee. I had fifteen cousins and never wanted for a playmate. Yet all the time in the background there was fear, a great simmering cauldron of paranoia and insecurity. We grew up with it, got so used to it that it was normal. It was a low level terror of political instability, the constant ebb and flow of poverty and violence in the streets that at any moment might spill over the threshold into our living room and consume us. An environment like that, it throws families in on themselves, for who else is there to rely on times of crisis?' Ash rested his head in his hands. 'This is all so difficult to talk about.'

'I am listening,' Isabella said simply.

'After I went to boarding school, I changed. It was a totally masculine environment. I didn't see a woman for months except the school nurse. When I came home in the holidays, I didn't know how to relate to my mother and sister.' He sighed. 'In becoming a man I amputated part of myself.'

Ash paused to sip his tea, giving himself a moment to collect his thoughts.

'History, politics, fear, religion, tradition, family, all of those things they make us who we are. In my case, they conspired to constrain my choices. When I was in Oxford, with you, I was a different person. For the first time in my life I was free to be myself. The way you were, Isabella, so independent, strong, kind and beautiful. When you played that violin, it made me bubble and fizz inside. I could almost forget India, the family, their expectations and my father's illness. But every time my mother's letters arrived I was drawn back in to their world. It was agonizing. I was turned inside out and ripped apart. I calculated that the easiest thing was to go along with my parent's wishes to find me a suitable girl. It was surreal. Perhaps part of me thought the marriage would never happen or that when I got back home that summer I could explain. But I was wrong. By the holidays my Dad's cancer had progressed. I was shocked. He came to the airport to meet me leaning on a stick, all skin and bone, his eyes sunk back in his head. He was living for my wedding and Ritu's family too was already deeply invested in the process.'

Ash sighed. 'It was such a whirlwind. Sure, the family were proud of me and overjoyed to have me home but no one really wanted to know about my life in Oxford. There was no sense that in that year in England I might have changed.'

'It sounds like you were a trophy son to be sold off.' Isabella couldn't help herself.

'In a way. But you should not judge my parents too harshly. It was their way of loving me. They were just doing what their parents did for them and their parents before that.' Ash swept up the crumbs from his plate with the side of his fork.

'Ritu and I were introduced in an Italian restaurant in New Delhi the day after my plane landed. I was barely over the jet lag. Italian! It was very expensive and a big deal. Ritu had never had eaten pizza before. She pronounced it over-rated. She liked music though. Her favourites were *Meatloaf, Queen* and *Lou Reed*. Very unusual taste for an Indian girl. I thought that boded well. It never occurred to me that she might be a lesbian. She had curled her hair prettily around her face and was well educated from a good family, very high caste, an excellent match. Years later, after our divorce, Ritu told me that ever since she was a little girl she had felt different, as if there were something wrong with her but didn't know how to articulate it. There was no such thing as a lesbian in 1970s and 1980s middle class New Delhi. The concept simply didn't exist. She thought that if she married an athletic hunk like me it would make her normal- her words not mine.'

'Poor soul.'

'Indeed. Ritu has been to hell and back over her sexuality. She finally came out to her family when she went to America and they didn't speak to her for years. Anyway, I could see that if I turned Ritu down there would be endless meetings with yet more girls. She was interesting and probably the best I was going to be offered, so I went along with it. But in the days before the ceremonies I couldn't sleep. All I could think of was you, Isabella, and the way you made me feel. I told my sister that I wanted to call off the wedding.' Ash laughed. 'She wacked me over the head with her slipper and told me not to be so bloody selfish. Her favourite word for me, selfish. Who the hell did I think I was? The house was buzzing. Relatives had come from out of town. We all had new clothes. My parents were so excited. A fortune had already been spent and what about her? If I jilted my bride, I would destroy my family's good name and with it her own marriage prospects. And didn't I realise, our father was dying? The shame would kill him. On and on she went, red faced with fury, whack, whack, whack with the slipper. In the end, I couldn't let everyone down. Don't laugh! You've never seen my sister. She's a tiger!' Ash wiped his mouth on a paper napkin and went on in a more serious tone.

'It's the way we were brought up as Indian men at that time. It all comes down to family honour.' He slapped his palms down on the table making the top jump up from the teapot.

'Ridiculous, in this day in age, you're right. But I knew my duty, what was expected of me; a successful career, an arranged marriage. It was, it is our way, the Indian way and we know how to make such marriages work. Hell, if I'd had a penny for every time someone has said that to me!' He smiled his lopsided smile and finished his tea. When his cup was empty he reached out across the table and took Isabella's hand in his, stroking her plain gold wedding ring.

'And the result of all this and Shiv's murder was that I learnt to supress my emotions. It was the only way I could cope. Once you have done that there are only two things left, power and money. And the casualty of all of this was you Isabella. I'm sorry.'

'Not just me,' she said quietly. 'The casualties were all of us.'

Isabella and Ash left The Tack Room and walked arm in arm down to the river, comfortable and quiet in each other's company. The sun was so low and bright that Isabella and Ash had to shade their eyes with their hands. A couple of college eights were out on the river, including a women's crew in blue college sweatshirts. Their coach rode along the towpath shouting encouragement through a megaphone, and the water splashed in crystal fountains off their blades.

When the time came for them to part, Ash walked Isabella back to the bus stop. Dusk was falling and the sky flamed orange and pink. They watched the bus coming, its headlights inching their way towards them in the traffic. Isabella's nose was red with cold but she couldn't find a tissue. Ash produced one, then put his arm around her shoulders and gave her a squeeze. She fiddled with her handbag looking for her bus ticket.

'It's going to be hectic for a while. I'll have to instruct a solicitor, keep the ship steady for the boys and I'm so behind with work. But next time I'm in London, may I buy you lunch?'

'Yes,' he smiled, 'I'd like that.'

A book is like a child. You can't bring it up alone. As ever, I am grateful to my family for their unwavering love and support. They make everything possible. Many people have helped with in various ways with kind words, gentle criticism, advice, introductions and encouragement. In particular I would like to thank Angela Barton, Jessica Finnis, Edgar Jenkins, Clare Kittmer, Kate Nash, Osama Siddique and the team at 2QT. Thank you everyone.

Rhiannon Jenkins Tsang is a British author whose work focuses on cultural and historical fault lines and has strong international themes. Rhiannon was born and grew up in Yorkshire and has studied, lived and worked in Europe and Asia. She read Oriental Studies (Chinese) at Oxford University and speaks Mandarin and Cantonese. Rhiannon lives in a former farmhouse in rural England with her family.

NOVELS

The Woman Who Lost China, Open Books 2013

The Last Vicereine, Penguin Random House 2017

SHORT STORY ANTHOLOGY

Hong Kong Noir, Akashic Books 2019

Twitter @rhiannonjtsang
Facebook Rhiannon Jenkins Tsang
LinkedIn Rhiannon Jenkins Tsang

Questions for Discussion
SPOILER ALERT
These questions are intended to enhance discussion after you have read the book. If you read them beforehand they might spoilt the story for you!

1. Each generation is a product of its time. Ash and Isabella were part of the nineteen eighties generation. What social, political and economic forces do you think influenced their choices and perspectives? What ideas and circumstances might have influenced your own generation? How do you think the youth of today will be affected by the Covid 19 pandemic?

2. The novel explores some of the potential complexities of inter-cultural and inter-racial relationships. Why do you think Ash was unable open up to Isabella about the pressure he was under to enter into an arranged marriage? Do you think he was right to keep her in the dark about it, and was his decision to go along with marriage the correct one?

3. Isabella had been living in an unsatisfactory marriage for many years before Ash returned. Why do you think she chose to stay in the marriage and was she right to do so?

4. How do you think Ash and Isabella matured and changed over time? If their older selves could meet their younger selves, what do you think they might say to each other?

5. After an itinerant childhood, Isabella found a place of peace, solace and inspiration in the Yorkshire Dales. Is there a place that means a lot to you and has influenced your life? What other novels have you read that might be defined by a keen sense of place?

Lightning Source UK Ltd.
Milton Keynes UK
UKHW011841210121
377470UK00002B/481